exposure

KIM ASKEW AND AMY HELMES

MeritPress

F+W Media, Inc.

Published by Merit Press
an imprint of F+W Media, Inc.
10151 Carver Road, Suite 200
Blue Ash, Ohio 45242
www.meritpressbooks.com

ISBN 10: 1-4405-5261-4
ISBN 13: 978-1-4405-5261-8
eISBN 10: 1-4405-5262-2
eISBN 13: 978-1-4405-5262-5

Printed in the United States of America.

10   9   8   7   6   5   4   3   2   1

This book is available at quantity discounts for bulk purchases.
For information, please call 1-800-289-0963.

Prologue

FOUR GIRLS IN ONE DORM ROOM. If it's not the very definition of hell, it's at least purgatory. Sharing a hundred and fifty square feet of living space in an ecru-painted cinderblock cell with three randoms, any of whom could turn out to have chronic Doritos breath, an unhealthy obsession with goth metal, or a tendency to slip into bizarre "baby talk" on the phone with her parents. School officials are forever insisting that roommate selection for incoming freshmen is completely arbitrary, but that never seems to explain how every dorm room ends up with a token weirdo.

For the residents of Room 315 in Birnkrant Hall, Skye Kingston was that girl. There was nothing overtly freakish about her, aside from the semi-creepy Diane Arbus photographs of circus midgets and identical twins plastered on the wall next to her bed. She was majoring in fine arts, with a specialty in photography, but "artsy" probably didn't entirely account for her singular personality; the way she seemed to hover attentively around campus like a studious fly on the wall.

Skye didn't resemble the Quasimodo-types typically identified—and ostracized—within the first few days of the semester. She wasn't mousy, overweight, or sporting an unfortunate excess of hormonally induced facial hair. Rather, her looks tended to land her on the other end of the hot-or-not spectrum, somewhere between "stunning" and "drop-dead gorgeous." She was model tall, with Eastern European features: long red tresses, pale skin, and glacial blue eyes that appeared, at once, both severe and serene. Hers was

3

an exotic beauty, in stark contrast to the tanned, toned bottled blondes with whom she shared tiny quarters on the dorm's third floor.

Whether or not she was cognizant of her good looks was up for debate. Her striking face was usually buried in a book—not hogging the bathroom mirror. She seemed to have a quiet confidence that was uncharacteristic of most of the freshmen girls who roamed the campus in lemming-like packs, thus singling her out out as an "untouchable." Upon occasionally emerging from the study lounge or library stacks, she'd peer out at the world through an ancient-looking 35-millimeter camera, avoiding direct eye contact with the unwashed masses of undergrads surrounding her. With a name like Skye Kingston, many presumed she had climbed straight off Daddy's yacht prior to arriving on campus. Others, including her roommates, had been speculating for weeks about the real story behind this mysterious freshman who defied classification.

"Did she live in an igloo or something?"

"No, you idiot. She's not an Eskimo!"

"I heard she lived in pitch black for half the year because the sun never rises there."

"That would explain the pasty-white skin."

"Well, I'd kill to have her skin, actually. It's like porcelain."

Skye sighed underneath her covers, listening to her roommates' gossip with a detached fascination. Like the Northern Lights in her native Anchorage, these Skye-centric chat sessions had become a nightly phenomenon, a fun pastime they routinely turned to after exhausting all of their catty comments about other socially condemned undergrads. Surely they couldn't think she'd be asleep already at quarter to ten, and even if she were sleeping, being openly conjectured about while she was less than four feet away was ludicrously ballsy of them.

"Maybe she's a vampire."

"Um . . . in that case, I'm putting in for a room transfer!"

"Well, supposedly she dabbles in the occult. That's what somebody in the caf told me at dinner yesterday."

"For real?"

"Yeah. Apparently she was involved with some lesbo coven of witches."

"Oh, come on, guys. You really don't think—"

"Some girl on the fourth floor heard from her R.A. that her boyfriend *murdered* a dude."

"No way."

"I'm serious. It was apparently all over the papers and stuff in Alaska."

"Holy shit."

Skye's heart began to race furiously underneath the covers. Being called "Ice Princess" and "Nanook of the North" was bad enough, but this time they were nearing a dangerous precipice with their idle gossip, threatening to reopen old wounds. She shifted underneath her blanket and cleared her throat. She hated confrontation—always had—but she had to at least let them know she could hear every word they were saying from her top bunk. Her movements prompted a shushing giggle down below.

"Uh . . . Skye? Are you awake?"

"What?" she said, knowing she was likely to regret it.

"You're from Alaska, right? And, well, it gets really cold there, right? And I'm wondering. . . . " the roommate could barely stifle her laughter. "Did your butt cheeks ever freeze to the toilet seat?"

The room below Skye's bunk erupted into self-satisfied cackles.

• • •

Sleep continued to elude Skye as her three roommates performed their fastidious evening bathroom rituals and finally clamored noisily into their twin beds. As she lay roasting underneath her blanket, she reflected on her bunkmates, who, so far, seemed to be the type of girls more worried about the intricacies of performing the perfect keg stand than such trivial matters as homework or attending class. She recognized the insecurity behind their conceit, and hoped that time would help soften their cutting edges. She had survived their brand of callousness before—barely, god knows. She didn't relish the thought of having to endure it all over again: the manipulation, the backstabbing, the selfish lust for power, the reckless disregard for people's feelings . . . people's lives.

Skye threw the blanket off her sweaty torso—Southern California was too hot for her—and took a deep breath. She hadn't planned on delving into her tumultuous past, but a candid discussion seemed in order. If laying all her cards on the table helped to break the ice, then it might be worth reliving the pain.

"'Murder' is a strong word, but not entirely off base," she said, breaking the dark silence. "If you insist on turning me into a movie of the week, I should at least provide you with some semblance of the facts."

She could hear the unsettled sound of sheets rustling and bedframes creaking, and saw the silhouette of one startled roomie as she sat up from her pillow.

"First, to answer some of your ongoing questions, the answers are, no: I've never seen Santa Claus. Yes: I *have* eaten reindeer meat, but it wasn't Rudolph. No: I would not strip for a Klondike Bar. And yes," she finally added, in a more stoic tone. "My boyfriend *did* kill someone . . . in a manner of speaking."

Skye stared at the ceiling three feet above her bunk. She had affixed glow-in-the-dark star decals there to remind her of home, forming the constellations of Ursa Major, Cassiopeia, and Orion. California's night sky was virtually a starless swath of smoggy gray. But looking at her artificial version of Alaska's heavens gave her little comfort. The perspective was all wrong. She was too close to the ceiling. You needed distance to really appreciate the staggering scope of it all. . . .

CHAPTER ONE

Fair Is Foul and Foul Is Fair

THIS TIME I HAD HIM IN MY CROSSHAIRS. Two more seconds and I'd take the shot.

"Hey, Skye! Over here."

Damn. I looked up through the throng of orange-and-blue-clad spectators to see Jillian Folger, the editor of our high school newspaper, waving frantically at me from the second row in the stands. Her brown curls bounced like springs as she waved, fittingly spastic hair for her hyperactive temperament.

As I returned my focus to the rink, the arena erupted into a cacophony of screaming voices.

"*GO RAVENS . . . !!!*"

Thirty-seven seconds left in the hockey game and we were tied, 4–4. The crowd was on its feet, and our archrivals, the Golden Grizzlies, were on the offensive attack. I should have been focusing on the players speeding across the ice like angry sharks in a giant tank full of chum. Instead, I took aim at Craig MacKenzie, who was still in the penalty box. High-sticking an opponent had earned him two minutes in the "sin bin," as it was sometimes called, and being a man down this late in the game was going to make it tough for us to clinch a victory in this first match of the season.

"*WE WANT BLOOD! WE WANT BLOOD!*"

The crowd was going primeval, but I was more interested in getting a closer look at Craig's gorgeous face through my zoom lens.

I didn't care about the game itself, which was practically sacrilege for a native Alaskan like myself to admit. Hockey here was the equivalent of football in Texas—a religion—which explained why our school had its very own ice arena on campus as well as "The Ice Girls," a squad of pinup-worthy skating cheerleaders who helped enliven (or should I say incite?) the crowd during timeouts.

"Now's your chance, MacKenzie! Annihilate them!" said someone standing a few rows behind me.

Craig was back on the ice now with eight seconds left on the clock. I gazed at him through my lens, stalker-like. He was taller and leaner than most of his teammates, with dark, wavy hair that fell over his green eyes in a charmingly cavalier fashion. Of course, you couldn't tell any of this through his armor of shoulder pads, shin guards, bulky gloves, and helmet.

Our star center, Duncan Shaw, grabbed my attention having just recovered the puck. He shot it with a forceful slap across the ice to a waiting Craig, who half-ran, half-skated toward the opposing goalie, elbowing a Grizzly defenseman out of his way before directing a shot that skimmed the goalpost and ricocheted into the net. With the click of a button, I caught Craig in his moment of triumph. His fists pumped the air just before the rest of his teammates piled onto him in celebration.

As our side of the rink erupted into cheers, I threaded my way over to Jillian.

"Talk about a clincher! This game's definitely destined for the front page," she shouted through the din. "Dream boy is going to be *everrrrr* so grateful when he sees your pics!"

Anyone would be happy to see their mug on the front page of the *Polar Bear Post*, but especially Craig. As much as I liked him, I also knew he was the kind of guy who couldn't pass a mirror without sneaking a glance.

Jillian and I made arrangements to meet at the newspaper office after school on Monday to lay out the issue. I headed gingerly onto the ice rink to where the team had convened for the typical self-congratulatory ritual of high-fives, back slaps, grunts, and play-by-play recaps. Craig was at the center of it all with Duncan, the senior team captain. With his white-blond hair and yoked physique, Duncan could have been cast as a Norse god in a Hollywood epic. My flair for fading into the woodwork made it easy for me to snap a few more photos of the sweaty victors.

"Nice save, bro! Granted, you hooked that guy good heading into the goal. I can't believe the ref didn't call the foul."

"What can I say, man?" Craig said, sounding barely winded. "Foul is fair, fair is foul. I knew he wouldn't send me back to the box with eight seconds left."

"Hey, I don't care if the ref needs laser eye surgery, as long as it works in our favor. Way to hustle, Mac!"

I was surprised to see Craig blush, but Duncan covered for him by pulling him into a headlock and slapping his helmet hard. Just then a chill traveled down my spine, and I realized that Craig's Gestapo girlfriend, Beth Morgan, and her loyal henchwoman, Kristy Winters, had swooped in right behind me on their skates (both were Ice Girls).

"Did you get what you were looking for?" Beth's sleek golden ponytail swung authoritatively behind her, as if it, too, had a major beef with me. Confused for a nanosecond, I actually felt guilty. For what, I wasn't exactly sure.

"The shots," Beth said, rolling her brown eyes toward their heavily shadowed lids. "Did you get any good shots of him?"

"Yeah, actually."

"I bet you did." Her knowing look made me feel, uncharitably, like scratching out her eyeballs, but I wisely refrained. Even though she was at least a head shorter than me, her ability to intimidate was on par with that of a trained assassin. Who knew a couple of bow-headed cheerleaders holding pompoms could look so threatening?

Beth motioned with her hand as if she was swatting away a fly, my apparent cue to step aside. I tried to do so without splaying myself across the ice. She brushed past me and practically leaped into Craig's arms, clutching him with heightened histrionics, as if he were Romeo, soon to be forever banished from Verona. You'd think they hadn't seen each other in months, when in reality it had probably only been two measly hours since their last make-out session. I couldn't seem to tear my eyes away from the horror of it all, but Duncan and the rest of the team acted totally indifferent to the blatant PDA as they mulled over plans for later that night. Apparently there was a postgame party over at The Hurlyburly Bar and Grill a mile from school. The food there was abysmal but it was an open secret that Easy Reynolds, the grizzled Vietnam vet who owned the joint, spiked glasses of Coke with bottom-shelf whiskey. In return for not checking IDs, he expected that a few extra tenners would be tacked onto his tip at the end of the night.

"Remember that time Duff tried to pay him in Canuck money and Easy went all PTSD on him?"

Kristy grimaced at the mention of her boyfriend, Duff Wallace. He was the team's power forward, but he was spending the semester in Edinburgh, Scotland, as part of a student-exchange program.

"He's probably not wasting any time thinking about us," she bellyached, evidently concerned that he was at that very moment kissing some winsome Scottish harpy.

Duncan shrugged his shoulders. "We're doing pretty okay without him, thanks to Mac's ability to channel Gretzky. Who knows? Duff might come back and find he's been dethroned!"

Kristy scowled. Beth smiled smugly. Craig's face held a mixture of pride and embarrassment.

As the team headed off the rink toward the locker room, I clumsily made my way back to terra firma. Fifteen minutes later as I was packing up my camera equipment, I sensed someone looming over me. I looked up to see our sports reporter, Leonard Livermore, smiling down at me with complete and utter adoration on his shiny face. It was probably the only time I'd seen him from this vantage point since he stood all of five-foot-two inches and I pretty much towered over him. On the social totem poll, he was equally diminutive, and yet he had a disproportionate level of self-confidence, at least where I was concerned. No matter how many times I rejected his romantic overtures, he seemed absolutely certain that someday soon I would throw myself into his welcoming arms as the dramatic score from some sappy romance movie reached an inspiring crescendo in the background.

The worst part about the whole situation was that bad breath, dandruff, and turbo-charged sebaceous glands aside, Lenny had a good heart. I felt like a total bitch for not requiting his ardent passion—after all, I fervently subscribed to the beauty-is-more-than-skin-deep philosophy. But there was no way Leonard and I were ever going to end up in a state of couple-hood. Not even my pinky finger could dredge up any romantic interest in the guy. I mean, even the poor guy's name was a turnoff. Since I couldn't find my way to being cruel—the only thing it might take to get him off my back for good—I had to play the tactful Elizabeth Bennet to his sniveling Mr. Collins on more than one occasion. Painful, to say the least.

"Hey, Lenny, I was just on my way to—" I stood up, peering around for the nearest exit and thinking of the best way to pull the ripcord on this conversation as quickly as possible.

"Skye, I really need to talk to you," he said, adding dramatically, "It's important."

Oh no. I quickly did a mental thumb-through of the excuses I could use for the upcoming weekend like watching my baby brother, finishing my project for art class . . . oh sweet Jesus—my social schedule wasn't exactly jam-packed.

"Can we talk on Monday, Lenny? I really need to go develop this film."

"Still living in the Dark Ages?" He often recycled this lame joke, referring to my stubborn resolve to use my dad's old camera instead of the digitals employed by everyone else in the free world. I loved the challenge of a 35-millimeter camera. Without the ability to review every shot, I had learned to trust myself. I treasured my time in the darkroom and the hands-on art of developing film. Granted, it took more effort to do it my way, but I was convinced that the results were worth it, even if it meant incurring the unbridled derision of everyone on the newspaper staff.

Lenny didn't wait for me to bat an eye, but instead took a deep breath and blurted out a phrase that still haunts my waking memory: "Will you go to prom with me?"

I was dumbstruck.

"But prom is *months* away," I said, stalling because I was utterly unprepared for this. "I can't really think that far ahead. It's only October!"

"Did someone else already ask you?"

"No, but. . . ."

"Then you'll go with me?" How was I going to get out of this one?

"Oh, Len, I'm way flattered that you would even think to invite me. But you know, you might change your mind between now and then. You might end up wanting to take some other girl, and, well, I'd hate for you to feel like you were already obligated to me."

Lenny examined me for a moment with a critical gaze. His frizzy, rust-colored hair sat like a molded Brillo pad on his head.

"So, presuming I don't end up wanting to ask anyone else, which I won't—duh!—then you'll go with me?"

"Uh . . . maybe we should play it by ear." It was hard to appear casual in the face of such a nightmarish scenario; still, I tried not to let him see the absolute look of unmitigated horror in my eyes. I didn't want to hurt his feelings, after all.

"Okay, I'll consider that a 'yes,' then, barring some unforeseen catastrophe, natural disaster, or change of heart on my part. Let me know what color dress you're wearing so I can color coordinate my cummerbund."

Color-coordination? Cummerbund? I'd really stepped in it now. At least I had almost seven months to hatch an escape plan. I grabbed my belongings and hightailed it out of there while Lenny stood grinning at me.

Letting the arena's glass doors swing shut behind me, I slung my camera strap over my shoulder and started across the parking lot. People were still filtering back to their cars, walking swiftly to avoid the crisp October air. They traveled in segregated packs: giddy freshmen girls with long, stick-straight hair, all dressed virtually alike in jeans, fleece-lined boots, and orange and blue knit scarves; the skater kids in their sweatshirts and jeans; and the band geeks lugging cumbersome trumpet cases.

"Oil gluttons!" screamed Jenna Powell from across the parking lot, addressing a trio of pretty boys as they piled into a massive SUV. Jenna was the president of the school's Green Team, and she took her eco-consciousness to an almost militant level. Whether being talked down from a birch tree she'd scaled in homage to her tree-hugging heroine, Julia "Butterfly" Hill, or organizing subversive "Ride Your Bike to School" rallies, Jenna's gung-ho, guerrilla-style tactics were a constant source of entertainment, and she often made the front page of the *Post*. That said, I respected her tenacity and thought her methods showed genuine creativity. Her intentions, at least, were always good, which is more than you could say for the huge oil companies she often railed against.

I could see my breath condensing in front of my face as I continued past the parking lot onto the school's quad.

"Wait up, Beanpole!"

My pulse sped up with excitement. My gawky stature had earned me lots of nicknames over the years, but only one person called me Beanpole. Not exactly your typical term of endearment, but nevertheless, it was music to my ears.

"Nice shot, Mac," I said, turning back to see Craig jogging to catch me. It was obvious from his damp hair that he'd just emerged from the locker room. He smelled yummy—like Irish Spring soap. Realizing I should say something else instead of breathing in his heavenly pheromones, I patted the camera by my side. "A true Kodak moment if ever there was one."

"I hope you got my good side!" As if he even *had* a bad side? "Where are you running off to?"

"The darkroom."

"It's past ten. Security will nab you sneaking in this late."

"*Au contraire* . . . Mr. Richter, the chair of the art department, believes that 'creativity cannot be confined to the hours between eight a.m. and three p.m.' He's made sure the art lab stays unlocked so that we can use it when inspiration strikes. You'd know this if you ever decided to suck it up and take an art class."

"You know I can't do that. It's not on the old man's master plan for my 'academic development.'"

"Does your dad think you're going to go insane and cut off your ear or something? It's just an art class."

"It's complicated."

I knew a few things about complicated. Like my friendship with Craig, for starters. Two years ago, I was one of the first people he had befriended when he moved to Anchorage from Illinois. He was, unquestionably, the cutest guy I had ever laid eyes on, and at the time, he was not yet clued into the high school hierarchy that pegged me a mere plebe. During the summer prior to the start of our sophomore year, we hung out almost every day, and the more I got to know him, the more I liked him. He was sweet, sensitive, and funny. We had everything in common, from our interest in art to our mutual obsession with Orson Welles films. I'd never really had a "best friend"—I was more the loner type. But getting to pal around with the new boy in town had opened my eyes to a whole world of possibilities, and I'd hoped, to something more than friendship.

I stopped in the shadow of our school's Gothic main tower, its crenellated roof line looming, castle-like, in the gloaming. Above the carved masonry of the entrance was a shield emblazoned with the words *Veritas Vincit.*

"Hang on a sec," I said. "The light right here is fiendish. I love it." I held my camera up and focused on the crest.

"Do you know what it means?"

"'Truth conquers.'"

"So you're a Latin savant, too?"

"Hardly. They drilled it into us during the world's most boring orientation the start of freshman year. Count yourself lucky you missed it."

Part of me always knew that first summer with Craig was too good to be true, and of course, I was right. Beth Morgan sunk her talons into him on the second day of school sophomore year, and there was no turning back. My dream scenario of being Craig's reason for living vanished overnight. I got demoted to the gawky "kid sis" while the marauding Miss Morgan was granted saliva-swapping privileges.

At first, I hated Craig for being blinded by the allure of the popular crowd. He was so much more interesting, so much smarter than they were! But we're all human, I suppose, and had Duncan Shaw deigned to show me any interest, I guess I would have followed as if he were the Pied Piper, too. It simply was never an option for me, but I couldn't exactly blame Craig for accepting his free passage into the cool clique.

"It's freezing out," he sighed, shoving his hands deeper in his jacket pockets.

"Wuss," I chided. "If you think this is bad, you'll never survive January."

We continued our pilgrimage diagonally across our school's quad, which was usually more tundra than lawn during the school year. We hadn't yet had our first big snowfall of the season, but the cold ground still felt like cement under our feet as we crunched over frosty remnants of grass. Anchoring the center of the quad was an immense spruce tree long known to students and alums as "Old Burny," allegedly because it was one of the few trees in the area to survive a devastating forest fire sometime back in the late 1800s. Wondering how far Craig intended on tagging along with me, I figured I ought to let him off the hook before things got too weird.

"Okay, well I'm going to go develop this film."

"Can I come?" I was more than a little surprised by his request.

"It's kind of a laborious process. Besides, aren't you going to the Hurlyburly?"

"They can spare a half-hour without me."

"Suit yourself."

To Craig's credit, he had never dissed me completely once he embarked on his upward social trajectory. He usually managed to offer up the perfunctory high-five in the hallway between classes or a cool "What's up, Beanpole?" when I passed his table in the cafeteria. We both recognized that he'd be risking social suicide to venture anything chattier than that. But occasionally, when he wasn't under the watchful eye of his gorgeous girlfriend or their rarified circle of friends, he and I could cut the bullshit and confide in each other again. It was almost like getting my old Craig back. Friends on the sly, you might say. If it bordered on pathetic that I cherished these brief encounters, so be it. I would take what I could get.

We made our way in silence to the school annex that housed the art lab. I could see a sliver of light coming from behind the industrial metal double doors. Pushing one door open and entering the room, I let out a small gasp of fright.

CHAPTER TWO

I Dreamt Last Night of the Three Weird Sisters

THE ART ROOM WAS EMPTY save for the three masked figures crouched in the middle of the fluorescent-lit room. Each wore an oversized head of papier-mâché: one featured a bulbous nose, beady black eyes and bushy eyebrows made of fake fur; one looked like a demonic raven with a twelve-inch pointed red beak and streaming feathers of dark red raffia; the final mask had a gaping mouth, protruding cheeks, and large hypnotic eyes.

The ghastly creatures were convulsing, hysterical with laughter. I immediately recognized the demonic raven thanks to the long dark, perfectly straight hair that cascaded over her shoulders.

"Cat, what are you guys *doing?*"

"Oh hey, Skye," Cat Ayuluk tried to collect herself as she cast off her mask. She was bright red from laughing and had to catch her breath. The streak of platinum blonde threaded through her dark hair shone like moonlight, reminding me of the song "Moon River" from *Breakfast at Tiffany's*. "We were just putting the finishing touches on our 'Myth and Perception' projects for Mr. Richter's mixed media class. They're due on Monday. You like?"

"Yup'ik masks," said Kaya Gilbert, who had just doffed her hell-mouth visage to reveal her heart-shaped face and razor-cut bob haircut.

"Those are pretty epic," I said. "Plus, Richter's gonna have to give you an A or risk appearing to be intolerant of your Alaskan heritage."

"That's the idea," said Tess Littlefish with a laugh. "Don't make the natives restless, dammit!"

Craig hung back in the doorway, ready to bolt if need be. I grabbed his arm and ushered him into the room. On the rare occasions when I touched him, it invariably triggered butterflies. This time was no exception.

"I'm dropping off the film from tonight's game. Craig scored the winning goal."

The girls stared at us blankly, completely disinterested in hearing more about the athletic prowess of my unhealthy obsession. I decided to try a different tack.

"You know, Craig here is a closeted Rembrandt, but I never could convince him to register for an art class."

"Too busy 'pucking' around?" Cat and Kaya gave Tess's pun a nod of appreciation.

The three girls had been thick as thieves since freshman year, their Eskimo ancestry functioning as the cement to their enviable bond. True purveyors of indie chic, they generally kept to themselves and steered clear of the high school milieu, but I had come to know them well, thanks to the AP classes we shared. I adored them, probably because, unlike yours truly, they didn't let the opinions of other people dictate their self-worth. They were edgy and cynical with an air of cerebral sophistication not often found in the average seventeen-year-old. Somehow, they seemed more enlightened than the rest of us, not counting their penchant for collapsing into laughter at their frequent inside jokes.

Craig didn't share any classes with Kaya, Cat, or Tess, which might explain his nervousness as he offered up some small talk. It was unusual to see him looking so like a fish out of water.

"Are these Eskimo masks? Or, uh, is it un-P.C. to say 'Eskimo?' I'm not as clued-in as I should be. Not originally from here," he stammered.

"You can call us anything, just so long as you *call* us—and, well, maybe let us drive the Zamboni," Tess said in a tone of mock flirtation. Though she had a lean, androgynous frame and boyishly short black hair, Tess was anything but a tomboy. Cat raised her eyebrows suggestively as she glanced in my direction. Sensing my mortification, she quickly covered.

"Our ancestors were Yup'ik people," she said. "One of their traditions was to carve masks like these for ritual dances. The masks were embodiments of a spiritual vision, and they were said to imbue the wearer with the spirit they represented. Here, try this one on for size."

Cat extended her red raven mask up to Craig's face. He peered through the eye slits and rotated his head slowly from left to right as he glanced about. He now seemed menacing, not the guy I'd been quietly lusting over for the last two years.

"The red color signifies royalty and power," Cat said. "The person wearing this mask is destined for a meteoric rise . . . a warrior king, perhaps."

"But beware," Kaya said, her hazel eyes glittering. "Red can also signify blood and death. Even the greatest of leaders are mere mortals."

"Sounds like shaman bullshit to me," Craig said with a laugh.

Cat yanked the mask away from his face. Her expression was a mixture of anger and hurt. I shot Craig a now-you-did-it glance and tried to diffuse the situation by reaching for Kaya's mask.

"Can I try? What's this one all about?"

"The wide eyes and the gaping mouth represent immortality," said Kaya, with an authority that belied her five-foot-one stature. "Whoever dons this mask will live on through the ages, never to fade away. Their greatness will increase with every new generation."

The mask felt perfectly molded to my face, and even a little constricting.

"That's too bad," I replied, removing the elaborate headpiece. "I kind of *like* being the walking wallflower of East Anchorage High."

"Oh, whatever, Miss-Legs-up-to-Your-Chin. You've got 'supermodel' written all over you, whether the idiot guys in this school know it yet or not." Kaya retrieved her mask from me and placed it on a metal shelving unit against the wall, alongside Tess's and Cat's.

"Who died and made *you* Anna Wintour?" I blushed. "Anyway, I think I'll stay behind the camera."

"Okay, we're outta here," said Kaya, grabbing her blue fleece parka. "Turn off the lights when you leave."

"No problem."

As the triumvirate headed out the door, it felt unsettling to be alone with Craig, especially following Kaya's random comment about me having model good looks. As if.

I headed toward the far end of the art lab to the darkroom (a.k.a. a glorified supply closet). About as anachronistic these days as rotary telephones and VCRs, I considered the darkroom my own private sanctuary. No one else ever used this space for its designated purpose, although I had twice walked in on Olympic-caliber tonsil hockey players going at it after school. I still shudder thinking about it. Those memories—experiences I had no firsthand knowledge of—made it all the more awkward to usher Craig into my inner lair.

He tossed his duffel bag in a corner of the tiny room and settled onto a wooden stool as I closed the door behind us.

"Never trust a woman who deals in hazardous material," he teased, pointing to the brown jugs of developing chemicals lined up on the shelf. A few unfurled spools of already-processed film hung streamer-like from various clamps set up around the small room where I'd earlier hung them to dry. "You know, you don't have to be so horse-and-buggy about it. Ever hear of digital cameras?"

"Not my style—I'm old school. Digital is so . . . predictable. When I develop pictures in a darkroom, it's almost like painting with light. There's a sense of mystery as the image slowly materializes in front of your eyes. It's a fascinating blend of science and art that is hard to describe. Besides, I like to be in control of things when I can. Now stay where you are and don't touch anything."

After scanning the table to make sure everything I needed was where it should be, I flipped off the overhead light and the room went pitch black.

"Why'd you do that?" Craig asked, a note of surprise in his voice.

"I'm transferring my film onto a developing reel," I said, already focused on my work. After removing the film from my camera, I pried apart the ends of the film cassette, careful not to touch the exposed surfaces of the filmstrip. Carefully, I wound the strip around the developing reel, making sure it spooled properly around the roll.

"But how can you see what you're doing?"

"I can't. If you expose the film to any amount of light, no matter how minute, the whole batch is pretty much ruined. Some people use a lightproof changing bag to transfer the film, but it's easier for me to feel my way in the dark. I really don't have to see to know what's what."

Whenever I was alone in the darkroom, I felt safe, like I was sheltered in a warm cocoon. Now, with Craig just a few feet away, I could hear him breathing and hoped that he couldn't hear my heart pounding like a stereo with a busted treble dial. The moment seemed rife with possibility.

Still groping in the dark, I placed the spool with its now-transferred film into the stainless steel developing canister and popped on the lightproof lid, then reached for the light switch. Instead, I accidentally flipped on the red safelight I used when making prints. Looking at Craig for a moment, his face was highlighted with red shadows. His eyes were pools of blackness . . . almost diabolical. Of course, I must have appeared equally *Dawn-of-the-Dead*-ish. The effect of the unnatural light was both eerie and intimate, as if we had suddenly been transported to some other freaky dimension.

"Whoops, wrong light," I said, flipping the safelight off and turning the regular overhead light back on. Craig winced at the sudden brightness as he snooped through a paint can full of red grease pencils.

"It's cool that you can have something that you're so into," he said. I reached past him to grab the bottle of developing solution.

"What do you mean? You have hockey."

"Yeah, I guess. But I'm talking about something more long term. I can't play hockey forever."

"I thought your dad had it all mapped out for you."

"Yeah. Go to Yale, pass the bar exam, then onto corporate law. Kill me now." He looked toward the floor, and pulled the drawstring at the bottom of his jacket back-and-forth, deep in thought. I replaced the cap on the unused bottle of developing solution—it could wait—and turned to give him my undivided attention.

"You know, Craig, you may find this hard to believe, but you are in control of your own destiny. Don't let anyone tell you otherwise."

"Thanks for the self-help seminar, but it doesn't quite work that way in the MacKenzie household."

"Yeah, well, God-willing, we'll all make it through to adulthood—we're in the homestretch, after all. You can make your own choices then, for better or worse."

That phrase made me think of Beth. Would those two actually get married some day or would he come to his senses first? I could picture her as a complete Bridezilla, barking orders to her bridesmaids as she marched down the aisle.

Craig began flipping through a binder that housed strips of my archived negatives, each tucked in plastic sleeves.

"I think your friends hate me," he remarked.

"What friends?" I said. "Oh, you mean Kaya and the girls?"

"Yeah."

"Don't sweat it. They can be a little abrasive at times, but they're totally cool."

"I still feel a little strange about the whole thing."

"Forget it, really. It's fine."

"No, I mean strange as in creepy. It's hard to describe, but when that tribal mask went up to my face, it felt intense . . . *weird.*"

No, I thought to myself. Weird would describe the way your axis-of-evil girlfriend insists on wearing three-inch heels to school when there's fifteen inches of snow on the ground.

I purposely avoided bringing Beth's name into any of my conversations with Craig. He rarely mentioned her, either. Call it a mutual understanding we had with each other. I suspected that he knew how much I reviled her. Maybe to some small degree, he reviled himself for dating her. In any case, discussing his succubus of a girlfriend wasn't within either of our respective comfort zones. Tonight, for some reason, was an exception.

"I showed Beth some of my still-life sketches the other day," he said.

"And . . . ?"

"Not exactly a rousing response from the cheering section."

"I don't get the impression Beth has the makings of an art critic. Your pictures are incredible."

"It was kind of demoralizing, though. I hardly show anyone those drawings. I guess I just thought she'd be more supportive."

"Well," I said, trying to be tactful, "I'm sure she brings other positive attributes to the table. Otherwise, you wouldn't be dating her."

"I guess there's a strength to her that I appreciate." He paused for a moment, then continued. "She's ambitious, and she's sure of herself, and she knows where she's going in life."

I realized that I didn't share any of those particular attributes. I was insecure and unsure about so many things.

"Holy hell, Beanpole, is that *me?*" he said, bending closer to the binder and pointing to a row of negatives. I looked closer.

"I don't know, let me see." I removed the strip of negatives from its plastic slot and held it up to the light. I knew it was him without having to scrutinize the portrait subject's dark skin and white, ghoulish eyes. "Yeah, that's you. That was from the scrimmage game a few weeks ago."

"God, I look *demonic.*"

"Everyone looks that way in a negative. But huh . . . *that's* funny . . ."

"What?"

"The way you've got your hockey helmet flipped back in this picture, it kind of looks like you're wearing a crown. You know, that's probably what Cat meant when she'd said you'd be a 'warrior king.'"

His face registered concern. "Yeah, but what about that death part?"

"Oh jeez, lighten up, Mac . . . it was only a papier-mâché mask!"

"But, I mean, it seemed like those girls, those friends of yours, sort of bought into the predictions. Do you think they were just putting one over on us?"

"I think it's pretty safe to say their so-called predictions were total B.S. But don't quote me on that. Besides, I kind of like what they envisioned for *my* future."

I carefully placed the negative back in its binder and put the developing tank with the film from tonight's game in a drawer for safekeeping. I'd come back to develop it on Monday morning. With Craig in here there was no way I could focus properly, anyway.

Craig grabbed his jacket and I opened up the closet door. As we headed for the exit, I stifled a yawn, but Craig seemed amped up.

"Want to come along to the Hurlyburly . . . help celebrate the win . . . grab a burger?"

My heart literally performed a double-twisting back somersault in my chest. He was inviting me to hang out? In *public*?! Was this actually happening?

"Really?" I half-swooned. "I don't know . . . who's gonna be there?"

"All the guys: Duncan, Brett, Nick, Sean . . . plus Beth, Kristy, Tiffany . . . probably some other Ice Girls."

He may as well have asked a baby sea lion to attend a Great White convention. I switched off the lights to the art room and braced myself for the Arctic chill.

"Hmmm. I've got to get up at the crack of dawn tomorrow to babysit my brother. I'd better just bag it."

"Maybe some other time, then."

I drove out of the school parking lot feeling a little bit trembly and numb, annoyed with myself in one respect and yet totally exhilarated. How is it that in one single night I managed to *accept* a total dork's invitation to the prom and also *decline* an invitation from the guy I was madly in love with? Naturally, I could never hang out with that crowd at the Hurlyburly. I would be absolutely paralyzed! But still . . . Craig had invited me! Not *exactly* immortality, to use Kaya's words—but a start.

CHAPTER THREE

How Now! What News?

WE WEREN'T EXACTLY the *Washington Post*, but that didn't stop Jillian from acting like every routine fire drill or addition to the cafeteria menu was a story of Watergate proportions. The girl was Lois Lane personified, ferreting out the most hard-hitting stories that could be mustered from an uneventful American high school like ours. She'd done investigative reports on the efficacy of Scantron machines at reading No. 2 pencils. She'd gotten an exclusive with the only celebrity alumnus (a no-name soap star) to ever attend East Anchorage High. She'd refused to reveal her source in a story about rampant graffiti in the second floor women's restroom after the principal, Mr. Schaeffer, ordered her to identify the tagger.

She could be nosy to a fault, incredibly crass, loud, and a little bit bossy, but to the staff members of the *Polar Bear Post*, Jillian was our fearless leader. As I sat at the computer mocking up the cover page for Wednesday's issue, she hovered over my shoulder, her brown springy tresses dangling just inside my peripheral vision.

"Your picture of Craig from the game Friday goes above the fold, Skye." She turned to look at my unwanted paramour working on the other computer in the office. "Leonard, write to half a page, and pad it if you have to."

"You're leading with sports *again?*" said reporter Megan Riordan. "But what about the debate team's trouncing of St. Mary's?"

Jillian sighed. "Did anyone sever their jugular at the microphone, Megan? If it bleeds, it leads, but otherwise, we stick with the fan favorites. The *New York Times* doesn't run a city council piece the morning after the Super Bowl. Did you interview Jenna yet about her run-in with the law over the weekend? That's the story I want to see."

Jenna Powell, our crusader for environmental *anything*, had made the local TV news over the weekend when she attended a downtown protest against the oil companies wearing a piece of duct tape over her mouth and not a stitch of clothing aside from some strategically placed dollar bills. It was only twenty-eight degrees outside at the time so, naturally, her wardrobe caused quite a stir. All day at school, people had been going up to her asking if she could spare some change.

"I'm keeping 'abreast' of the situation," joked Megan, which garnered a droll 'hardee-har-har' from the rest of us. Jillian returned the focus to the issue at hand, literally.

"Editorial page. Who's got ideas?"

"College acceptance angst?" Typical Megan, jonesing for another byline.

"Uggh. Thick envelope? Thin envelope? It's already cliché and it's only October."

The very mention of the topic made my heart hurt a little. It would soon be time to start submitting college applications, and the entire process was both daunting and dreadful. I had my A wish list and my B wish list, and even my "resign yourself to a life of jobless obscurity" C wish list. Grade-wise, I had what it took, but paying for it all was going to require climbing a beanstalk and beseeching a sinister giant to front my tuition. My dad had reassured me that we'd find a way to make it work, but I knew behind his chipper façade that money was tight, and that, for a variety of reasons, I might still end up trading Ivy League for bush league: a local community college.

Still wracking our brains for a column idea that would win Jillian's approval, Lenny leaned precariously back on the legs of his desk chair, seemingly much better at courting a spinal cord injury than courting me.

"What about 'Do You Believe In Miracles?: East Anchorage's Dream Team,'" he said.

"Last time I checked our banner did not read *Sports Illustrated*."

"Oh I'm sorry, Megan, did you say something? I fell asleep there for a second reading your last article on the broken vending machine. Ground-breaking stuff." Megan and Lenny's distaste for one another occasionally flared up into these momentary spats. Sensing an opportunity to get Craig some more good press, I opted to choose sides.

"I think Lenny's got a good point. Nobody expected the Ravens to be contenders this season. Everyone's been talking about it."

Lenny beamed at me, lovestruck, as if I'd just announced that I wanted to meet him under the bleachers after class. I'd be paying for this later, I was sure.

"True," conceded Jillian, pushing a chunk of hair behind her ear. "The guys at the *Daily News* are already predicting they could take all-city this year."

It was fairly typical at our weekly staff meetings for Jillian to invoke the sacred name of the *Daily News*, Anchorage's city paper at which she'd been participating in a work-study program for the past six months. Her reverence and idolatry for the journalists was comical at times but, on occasion, her access to their reportage had helped us publish some noteworthy gems. Jillian liked to remind us that she was connected to the big boys.

"And they're doing it all without Duff Wallace on the team," I added. "Craig really filled the void and surprised everyone."

"Okay, we'll go with that angle then. Lenny, you know what to do." Jillian's eyes narrowed as if struck by another thought. "Speaking of Duff, I think there's another story there. Apparently a marked interest in seeing the world was *not* what prompted him to sign up for a semester in Scotland. I have it on good authority that he needed to get the heck out of Dodge. Lawyers were involved. Keep your ears open on that one and see what surfaces. And don't forget! Next week is Halloween! Skye, get as many costume shots as you can."

As I packed up my army green corduroy messenger bag and headed for the exit, I heard my wannabe lover's voice echo behind me.

"I can't wait to see what *you'll* be wearing, Skye. Maybe Jenna'll lend you her protest ensemble for a costume?"

He meant to be flirting, I suppose, but poor Lenny didn't have the kind of face that made a comment like that permissible. Had Craig said it, I would have blushed and melted into a puddle before gushing about it in my journal. Coming from Lenny, it was ten kinds of wrong.

CHAPTER FOUR

Full of Sound and Fury, Signifying Nothing

OUR AP CALCULUS TEACHER, MRS. SHERIDAN, was in a state of rapture as she scribbled out the solution to a function on the blackboard. Crumbling bits of chalk ricocheted off the board in her frenzied pursuit of mathematics ecstasy. Jarringly, she was dressed up as Raggedy Ann, wearing candy-striped tights, bloomers, a floral dress and apron, and a red yarn wig.

My classmates, too hopped-up on sugar to be paying any attention today, were focused on the clock, waiting for the trembling minute hand to click directly vertical. When it did, we immediately started loading up backpacks and raucously sliding our chairs back from our desks, unconcerned with the fact that Mrs. Sheridan hadn't yet finished her problem. Knowing it was futile to continue, she yielded to the mass exodus of costumed figures with an exhausted smile on her faux-freckled face.

"See you tomorrow, class. Don't forget about the quiz we have this Friday."

Grabbing my cane and bowler hat, I funneled up the row of desks heading for the door but was stopped in my tracks.

"Skye. Question."

I looked down at Beth, who was still seated at her desk and checking herself out in a powder compact. What was it about Halloween that gave every girl license to dress as slutty as possible?

She was wearing a red bustier, shiny vinyl hot pants, and fishnet stockings. Two glittery horns protruded from her headband. You'd think she was lobbying for Playmate of the Year. Beth snapped her compact shut in a businesslike fashion and deigned to make eye contact with me.

"Did you read the next chapters for lit class?"

I'll admit that it was one of the facts about Beth that irked me the most: aside from being beautiful, popular, and the undeserving girlfriend of the only guy I'd ever cared about, she actually, I hated to confess, had a brain in her head. Shocking, I know, but we shared a lot of the same advanced-level classes.

"Yeah, I read it over the weekend."

"Perfection. I was over at Craig's for a lot of the weekend, and so, as you can imagine, I just didn't have time to skim it. I was hoping you could give me the basic gist on our way to class. You know, in case Phyllis calls on me?" Beth had the insouciance to call our teachers by their first names.

"Well, I mean, it's *The Sound and the Fury*—William Faulkner is tough to condense into talking points. It's pretty enigmatic."

"Never mind then," she said, looking annoyed. "I guess I'll just fake it."

It was something she was highly proficient in. Her whole high school career had been about faking it. Her popularity was built on an elaborate ruse to make people forget where she came from and force them to only focus on where she was going.

Certainly her looks and her attitude all screamed upper crust, but I knew better. She and I had gone to grade school together. We'd been in the same Girl Scout troop and the Brownies before that.

I'd seen the beat-up, hubcapless, seventies-era Chevy pick-up truck that her dad drove to the docks every day. He worked as a longshoreman when he wasn't out to sea for weeks at a time during crab season. Beth's mother had died when she was eleven, so now it was just her and her dad. It must have been lonely for her, in a lot of respects, but she never let on that there were any chinks in her armor. She was evidently a master at stretching a dollar, always coming to school looking polished and fashionable. I suspected she borrowed threads from more well-to-do friends like Kristy, and I'd even heard that she got a small stipend of spending money from her dad's brother, who owned a chain of movie theaters in Anchorage.

No one would have judged Beth for any of this. Seventy percent of the kids in school were from blue-collar stock, including yours truly. But she insisted on pretending that she was no different than any of the "black gold" crew: the kids whose fathers did big business for the oil companies. Craig's father was one of these men, having been transferred here to spearhead exploratory research while the Feds debated whether or not to allow drilling in the Arctic National Wildlife Refuge.

Speaking of wildlife, Beth's furrowed brow and glowering eyes combined with her thick application of liquid eyeliner currently made her resemble a bird of prey.

"You know, Craig always tells me that you're a sweet girl, which is why I thought I could ask you for help, but I see that I was wrong. Or maybe *he* was."

I so did not want to be having this discussion. I could tell that there was going to be no way to extricate myself painlessly from the conversation. Behind her on a bulletin board was a too-precious motivational poster of a kitten hanging from a tree limb. I took its message, "Hang in there," to heart.

"Well, Craig *has* been known to have bad judgment about certain things, that's true," I disingenuously replied. Beth's blonde head reared back ever so slightly, as if she weren't sure whether to take this as a personal affront or not.

"It's fine to have a crush on him, Skye—most girls do," she sighed. "But if you're harboring any Disney-style delusions about being his hideous, taffeta-clad prom date come spring, you can purge yourself of those grand fantasies right now."

First Lenny, now Beth. What was it with everyone and prom? "He and I will naturally be Prom King and Queen," she said, glaring up at me. "So you'll just have to content yourself with being his fawning fool, which is pretty much what you look like whenever you're mooning over him from a distance."

The thought of anyone giving a crap about wearing a fakey rhinestone princess crown in a badly decorated gym was laughable to me. I wished I could have delivered one of those cutting one-liners that I always managed to think up hours after the fact when I replayed the conversation in my brain. Instead, the left portion of my fake mustache had chosen that exact moment to slip down over my lips. I forgot I'd been wearing it and now felt even more foolish. Beth smirked, grabbed her plastic trident, and sashayed out of the classroom. As she exited, the red felt tail attached to her belt swung like a decisive pendulum.

• • •

Old Burny's ancient branches cast an appropriately eerie shadow over the quad as I made my way toward the school parking lot. I was eager to get home and see my baby bro, Oliver, dressed up like Yoda. My dad was a rabid *Star Wars* geek and had found the cutest pair of costume Yoda ears online, but I knew my brother was likely to keep them on for all of two minutes before he'd start to get fussy and recalcitrant about the whole thing. I wanted to get some pictures of him before that happened. The sky was beginning to turn the color of a bruise. Purples and grays swirled together as the sun glowed red behind the clouds. Already the days were getting shorter. By December we'd be down to only five-and-a-half hours of daylight. The wind cut against my cheeks and I pulled up the lapels on my oversized men's suit borrowed from Dad's closet. I think he'd worn it only twice: to a funeral and to a job interview. It still smelled new.

"Hey, tramp!"

I glanced over and saw Cat unlocking the trunk of her car. Tess and Kaya tossed in their boulder-sized backpacks. All three were wearing nylon witches' hats, the kind you might pick up in the costume aisle of a drugstore. Apart from that, they were decked out in their typical dark denim jeans and ironic T-shirts layered over thermals, the epitome of hipster nonchalance. I felt overdressed in my suit.

"Charlie Chaplin," said Tess, grabbing for my pocket hankie and teasingly waving it at me. "Nice 'stache!"

"We're going to the midnight showing of *Rocky Horror* over at the Regent tonight," said Kaya. "Want to come?"

"Thanks for the invite, but my dad is still into the militant curfew thing on school nights."

"How charmingly provincial of him. Well, the offer's out there if you can bust outta Alcatraz."

"Thanks," I said with laugh, before retrieving my hanky.

As Cat shut her car trunk, a posse of our school's A-listers walked past surrounded by their various groupies and hangers on. Oh God . . . was Beth right? Did I look like those chumps fawning over Craig? In the middle of the pack, I noticed him, his hair combed into an outrageous pompadour. He wore a white bejeweled bell-bottomed jumpsuit with a huge collar, and he sported the trademark gold-rimmed shades.

"Hey, hey, li'l darling," he drawled, pointing in my direction and striking a wide-legged stance. "Why don't you go on and make me a peanut-butter-and-banana sandwich?"

Tess and Kaya had already gotten into the car, and as Cat opened the driver's side door, she remarked on Craig's costume.

"Looks like we had you pegged. You *were* destined to be 'King.' That Yup'ik mask, man—it doesn't lie. Let's hope, for your sake, the predictions end there."

She entered the car, slammed the door shut, and all three girls gave us a friendly wave as they pulled out of their parking spot. They were still wearing their witch hats, which were bent over under the roof of the car.

Craig removed his sunglasses and watched them drive down the road. He didn't say anything for a few seconds, and since I'd already been feeling awkward about our last conversation in the darkroom, I tried to break the ice as his groupies slowly dispersed.

"Where's Beth?"

No answer. He was still looking off at where Cat's car had turned out of sight; Elvis rocking it pensive-style.

"Did she go to hell?"

Craig turned and looked at me, confused.

"What? Who?"

"*Beth*."

"Why would you say something like that? That's not cool."

"Uh, she was dressed as a *devil*. It was a joke, Mac, jeez!"

"Oh. Right. She actually went home sick this afternoon. She threw up in gym class."

"Oh, that's too bad. I hope she feels better."

More silence. This was weird. The sky already seemed darker now than it was five minutes ago. I peeled off my mustache and quickly stashed it in my messenger bag. Craig reached over and rubbed off some of the sticky residue from my upper lip, causing my face to instantly flush. Was he seriously wiping off my mustache boogers? I looked down toward the blacktop rather than make eye contact with him, but eventually glanced back up. I couldn't tell if the smile on his face meant anything other than, "You look ridiculous," but it seemed like it could have. I blushed again, but thankfully he didn't notice. Duncan was yelling to us from across the parking lot.

"Yo, numbnuts! You want a ride or not?"

Craig's jawline visibly tensed. He and Duncan had become pals pretty quickly on the heels of his debut at school two years ago, but there was definitely a pecking order to this friendship. As much as Duncan seemed to enjoy Craig's company, he occasionally seized the opportunity to show him—and everyone else—who was the alpha male. Craig usually tried to laugh it off, but I think it bothered him more than he let on.

"What?" he yelled back. "Is your crap car going to turn into a pumpkin in thirty seconds?"

Duncan grinned and started casually striding in our direction, tossing his keys up in the air and catching them every few steps.

"Whatever, bro. I don't exactly see *you* driving a luxury vehicle and god knows your pops could afford it. Dude, I'm sick of waiting around for you to wrap up this session of 'geek love'—no offense, Skye—so let's motor. I've got three hours of SportsCenter to veg on before my mom gets home and pries my ass off the couch."

Craig gave me an apologetic look, then used both hands to mash my bowler hat down over my face. By the time I'd righted it and could see again, he was jogging in his white jumpsuit toward Duncan's car.

CHAPTER FIVE

It Is a Knell That Summons
Thee to Heaven or to Hell

LATE TO SCHOOL YET AGAIN, I skidded in my Chuck Taylors, rounding the corner of the fluorescent-lit hallway only to run smack into Craig, who reached out to steady me. Not in time, unfortunately, to stop my books from tumbling to the tile floor in total disarray.

"Whoa, Beanpole! Where's the fire?" He grinned before bending to help gather up my scattered belongings.

"Overslept," I said, while trying to accomplish a couple things at once: checking out how adorably hot he looked in his blue T-shirt while also reaching over to pick up my green leather journal before he could spot it. "What about you? Shouldn't you be in homeroom?"

"I have thoroughly convinced half the staff of this high school that I suffer from an overactive bladder," he said, digging his cell phone from the front pocket of his jeans. "Pretty much gives me *carte blanche* to roam the hallways at will. Right now I'm arranging refreshments for tonight's festivities. There's a party out at Kristy's dad's hunting shack." He ran one hand through his dark wavy hair and started dialing with the other. "You should come."

"Sounds like a teen slasher movie in the making." I couldn't hide my sarcasm. "Trapped out in the middle of nowhere with a bunch of Future Frat Boys of America, not to mention Beth Morgan. I'm not exactly her favorite person, you know."

"You should give them a chance," he said. "You might be surprised. . . . Yeah, can I speak to Mick," he said into the phone as he reached down to pick up a stray sheet of paper. "Or, you could go to this instead." He held up the invitation to Jenna's monthly, and poorly attended, Power to the People Potluck. Rolling my eyes, I reached out to snatch the flyer back. He held it—and my gaze—for about two seconds too long. Then he let it go, turned, and walked out the door to the quad just as the morning bell started to echo through the hallway.

As Friday morning classes wore on I became more and more vexed about my encounter with Craig. Even Mr. Richter's lecture on Man Ray in fourth period failed to distract me from my inner turmoil. How *dare* he continue to pull these "come one, come all" invitations to hang out with his posse, as if I were really welcome? As enticing as it sounded, I figured I'd better pass for the sake of my own sanity and self-preservation. Besides, who knows what I'd say to Craig after guzzling a drink or two? No way did I want to live that down for the rest of the foreseeable future. Still, I was making it just a little too convenient for him to smile and pat me on the back with that "Beanpole" act of his. As if his offer was genuine when we both knew I would never actually take him up on it. Was this his way of feeling less guilty about our pseudo-friendship and the way he'd dropped me with barely a backward glance? And now to pretend that being the odd-girl-out was my own doing. . . . How thoroughly would he *freak* if I should happen to call his bluff? I knew that it would be asking for trouble, but I didn't have a whole lot to lose at this point. I'd swooned over "Golden Boy" long enough. Now, I decided, I wanted to make him squirm.

• • •

I'd concocted a solid enough plan by the time the noon bell rang, but it was going to require faking my way through some tremendously uncomfortable moments. When I casually strolled over to his crowded table at lunchtime, I felt like Marie Antoinette proudly stepping up to face the guillotine.

"Hey, Craig. Just wanted to let you know that my plans for tonight fell through, so I would love to take you up on your offer to come to the party."

The dismayed, mouth-agape look on Beth's face was priceless. So far, so good. I held my head up a bit higher now even though I sort of felt like peeing my pants.

Craig placed his half-eaten slice of pizza on his plate and wiped his mouth as the rest of his table waited, like loyal subjects, for him to respond. He could barely look at me as he unenthusiastically replied.

"Umm . . . okay then. See you there."

"Where?"

"What?"

"Where's the party? You never gave me an address."

He concentrated intently now on the wavy white line on his Coke can. Beth wasted no time in shanghaiing the conversation.

"Oh Skye, it's superrrrr far from here and the directions are soooo confusing. I wouldn't even know how to explain it to someone who's never been."

What would Leonard Livermore do in a situation like this? If my tentative prom date had taught me anything, it was how to win an argument with unflappable confidence and blatant disregard for the chill in the air.

"Hmmm," I said. "Well then, in that case, it might just be easier if I hitched a ride there with you guys. Craig, you know where my house is. Why don't you just swing by on your way?"

Beth was about to protest, but I saw Craig grab her hand and give it a squeeze, as if reining her in. He mustered a weary smile for me. "Can you be ready at eight thirty?"

"Of course! See you guys then. Can't wait!" Before I turned jauntily on my heel I saw Beth shoot Craig one of her furrowed brow specials.

• • •

My dad chopped organic carrots for Ollie's baby food while I sat at the kitchen counter, a dozen lipsticks pilfered from my mom's makeup drawer arrayed in front of me like pirate booty. She was working the late shift at the Regent, the oldest and best of Beth's uncle's movie theaters and the only one that showed classic films like *Philadelphia Story* and *Casablanca*. When Craig first moved to Anchorage, a noir film series was in full swing and we spent hours, elbow to elbow, in the darkened theater watching sultry scenes between Humphrey Bogart and Lauren Bacall, Jimmy Stewart and Grace Kelly. I could hardly believe the guy I shared Red Vines with back then was the same person who had so grimly accepted my ostensibly bold R.S.V.P. hours earlier.

I carefully applied a cherry-red shade using the silver toaster as a makeshift mirror and was relieved to notice that the zit-zapper cream I'd been applying all week had finally destroyed most of the freakishly large pimple sitting rakishly astride my left nostril. Despite this glimmer of good news on the complexion front, I was not in the best frame of mind to take advice—especially from my dad, who I was fairly certain had absolutely no clue what it was like to be me. If the ink-filled pages of his yearbook were any indication, he'd spent the better part of high school basking in the unadulterated admiration of everyone from fellow jocks to drama geeks. He and my mom, former high school sweethearts, were always after me to be myself. I know they meant well, but really, how cliché can you get? It's easy to be yourself when everyone thinks you're the greatest thing since sliced bread.

"Skye, I know I'm not supposed to say this," Dad said, "but when it comes to teenage boys, I think you shouldn't be above playing hard-to-get."

Sometimes I appreciated the fact that my dad was comfortable enough to talk to me about anything—and I mean *anything*. This was not one of those times. Now that I had to face the repercussions of my inspired lunchtime performance, I could feel my confidence take a slow dive. It was going to be a long and trying night for me, and I was attempting to shore up my tough-girl exterior to hide how terrified I really felt. I looked up at my dad and scoffed.

"First of all, like I've told you a couple million times already, Craig and I are just friends. And secondly," and here's where I really screwed up, "why don't you try taking your own advice for a change?" Dad looked stricken and Ollie, as if in protest, began to howl.

It was a low blow and I knew it. My mom had recently gone back to school to study medicine and my dad had become a veritable Mr. Mom, taking care of Ollie and the house when he wasn't working as the manager at a hardware store. I helped out too, when I could spare the time from school, homework, and the paper. At first it seemed to be working out great, but then Mom started clocking more hours with her study group. Between that and her part-time job at the Regent, she was spending less and less time with us. The harder my dad tried, the farther away she seemed to get. When I slammed the front door shut on the way out an hour later, I was still giving Dad the silent treatment as if he'd actually done something wrong, rather than the other way around.

Beth didn't even attempt to push her seat forward as I squeezed in behind her and tumbled into the back seat of Craig's Jeep

Wrangler. Ever in a state of denial, Craig tried to pretend like the situation was one hundred percent normal. At least Beth had the dignity to be honest about her feelings. She certainly didn't attempt to veil her disgust with me as we merged onto the highway that led out of town. The ride was strained, to say the least, and her occasional grimaces in my direction were reminiscent of a teenage Medusa. She used every opportunity to blatantly caress Craig's leg or entwine her manicured fingers in his hair while giving me tight-lipped smiles that seemed to say, "Jealous much?" She even rolled down her window completely to blast me with arctic air while she tapped the ash of her cigarette into the wind.

"Oh, is that too much air for you, honey?" she said, when she saw my now-knotted red hair plastered against my face. "I didn't want to bother you with my smoke."

Turning onto a winding rural road, we careened over icy patches as the outline of snow-covered trees, illuminated by the headlights, narrowed in on us. I could swear I saw the glowing eyes of some forest creature—a moose no doubt, or perhaps some enormous she-wolf—peering at us ominously from the depths of the forest. Whether inside or outside the car, I was not in safe territory. When we reached the end of a long sloped driveway, my relief at having finally arrived was short-lived. A warm, but not welcoming, bonfire raged in front of the cabin. Every window of the old domicile was lit up, and the silhouettes of drunken seventeen-year-olds made me sigh in trepidation. These people obviously didn't have a care in the world. I couldn't even begin to imagine what that must have felt like.

CHAPTER SIX

That Which Hath Made Them Drunk
Hath Made Me Bold

TYPICALLY I'D ONLY OVERHEARD TALES of the epic parties held here as they were retold during hasty Monday morning postmortems. Details would emerge in hushed tones at the back of the rancid-smelling senior study hall presided over by an overscrupulous and ancient guidance counselor, Mr. Kirkpatrick, who still threw around words like *skullduggery* as if they were part of your average twenty-first-century teen's lexicon. Now, I'd actually stepped over the threshold and into the crème de la crème of East Anchorage High's party central.

All was confusion and noise as my eyes adjusted to the room; that too-familiar feeling of panic rose and I knew instantly that my skin was probably the crimson shade of a boiled lobster. Luckily it was too dark inside for anyone to see much, and anyway, everyone was apparently utterly bewitched by über-couple Craig and Beth whose big entrance preceded my inconsequential one. Damn, you'd think they were royalty or something the way everyone seemed to bow and curtsey in their presence.

My first thought was that even though I'd only ever heard the place called a "shack," it was really a sprawling conglomeration of rooms that branched off from what had evidently been the original homestead. I didn't know how many rooms there were, but at least three doors led away from the small shack into other parts of the structure that, judging from what I could see, must have been added on in different decades. Scattered throughout were abandoned pieces of furniture. Here a stained couch gradually losing its stuffing, there a rickety table and stool. Empty, it would make an excellent spot for a photo shoot. A beer can flew across the room, landing on a pile in the corner.

"Hey," someone in the crowd joked, "better recycle that or Jenna will have your ass!"

"Craig!" Duncan waved from a corner of the room looking more brawny and barrel-chested than ever. I tried to act nonchalant as I shadowed Craig and Beth over to where Duncan stood surrounded by a rapt group of freshmen and sophomores, including the vapidly pretty Tiffany Towers, his girlfriend-of-the-month and the police chief's daughter.

"No paparazzi allowed." Duncan flashed a quick smile to let me know he was joking, but when he glanced at Beth, his smile faded.

Under her breath, Beth hissed, "Skye, maybe you should go make some new friends."

Craig looked the other way, pretending not to hear.

Feeling like a complete jackass, I slunk off, mortified and hating myself for letting Beth have all the power once again. As I crossed the threshold into the next room, I tripped over a keg hose and ended up face to face with Beth's best friend, Kristy. Just my luck to step out of the frying pan and into the fire, I thought.

"Drink this," she said, handing me a neon green Jello shot. I tossed it down as if it was something I did every Friday night.

"Don't let that bitch get to you." She stared pointedly in Beth's direction.

I must have looked completely floored because she added, conspiratorially, "My grandfather used to say, 'You never really know your friends from your enemies until the ice breaks.'"

"Uh huh," I said, totally wondering what the hell *she'd* been drinking.

"I learned a few things today about my so-called best friend." She nodded in the direction of the Wicked Witch of East Anchorage. "And when she least expects it, I'm going to enjoy making her pay."

"What did she do to *you*?" I was expecting Kristy to say that Beth had shrunk her Prada miniskirt or lost her string of loaner pearls, the typical cheerleader bullshit.

"I just found out she's the reason Duff got shipped off to Scotland."

"*Beth* did that? Why? How'd you find out?"

"That's classified info, but consider yourself lucky that you don't have a boyfriend. If you did, I'm sure Beth would be after him, too."

Little did she know that as far as I was concerned Beth had already pretty much stolen the closest thing I'd ever had to a boyfriend.

"Want to know something totally effed-up?" Kristy flipped her long, perfectly highlighted hair over one shoulder and leaned in to whisper. "Craig doesn't know this, but she made a pass at Duncan last week. He wouldn't have anything to do with her."

"But she and Craig—" I started to protest.

"She doesn't really care about Craig, or anyone else for that matter. She's just a sociopathic social climber. She should wear a sign: 'Prom Queen or Bust,'" Kristy said, delighted with her own joke. She spun around, a little unsteadily, and vanished into the shadows of the adjoining room.

I wasn't naive enough to think that Kristy had taken me into her confidence because she recognized friend material. The fact that Beth openly despised me made me the obvious choice for passing on any damaging rumors about her. Clearly Kristy had handpicked me to start spreading the gossip about Duncan. Even if it was true—and it probably was just Kristy on a revenge mission for whatever she believed had happened with Duff—I wasn't going to stoop to her level. Frankly, it was none of my business. Besides, I was finally starting to believe that Craig and Beth deserved one another.

Left to my own devices and feeling a tad buzzed from the shot, I decided to explore the party scene, with the certainty that my presence would go virtually undetected; a detached anthropologist observing the mating habits and group dynamics of popular kids in their natural habitat, I mused. At least I could make fun of the whole thing later with Kaya and the girls.

In the hallway, an open bathroom door revealed the same intrepid freshman I'd seen displaying beer bong bravado when we first arrived; he was now crouched in front of the toilet in woeful misery.

"Mom?" he muttered pitifully as I passed by. Well, even if he's delusional he can still speak, I thought, and made a mental note to check on him again in fifteen minutes. I needed a moment to decompress and get a handle on what had already happened tonight. I considered calling my dad, but even if my cell phone had worked out here in the middle of nowhere— which it didn't—I was too ashamed to ask him to bail me out after the way I'd acted. I did what I usually do in uncomfortable situations, which was to take framed imaginary shots of my surroundings in my head.

I felt a tap on my shoulder and turned around to see Craig standing behind me.

"Hey, Beanpole." He looked embarrassed. "I've been looking for you."

"Doubtful." That felt good, I thought, and stood a little taller.

"Look, I'm sorry about earlier. . . . "

"Sorry for ignoring me, or sorry for inviting me in the first place?"

"For acting weird. I was just surprised you even accepted, that's all."

"Oh, so you *were* just patronizing me. Thanks for clarifying."

"That's not what I mean. I'm glad you came, really." He lowered his head a few inches so that his eyes peered directly into mine. There was a glint in his green orbs that seemed to both flirt with me and beg my forgiveness, pretty-please-style, with a cherry on top. Damn, he was cute. But I was probably imagining the flirting part.

"Forget it." My pride caved instantly to my passion. "You don't need to apologize for anything."

"No, really, Skye." It surprised me to hear him say my real name. He looked into my eyes and—I kid you not—we must have stood like that for fifteen seconds while the blur of the party circled around us. Crammed into the room like we were, our faces were mere inches apart. I couldn't blink, I couldn't speak . . . I don't think I even breathed.

He grabbed my hand and whispered, "Let's go somewhere where we can talk."

Just then someone yelled "flashlight tag!" and I turned to see Beth armed with two flashlights, pushing her way toward us through the dispersing crowd like a salmon swimming upstream. Craig dropped my hand and mumbled, "Later, okay?" as Beth tossed me one of the flashlights. Pulling Craig along behind her without a backward glance, she made for the door.

CHAPTER SEVEN

What's Done Cannot Be Undone

FLASHLIGHT TAG IS A PRIMAL GAME, pitting the hunter against the hunted. In the wilds of Alaska, one might prefer to be discovered early on, for the longer the hunt continues, the scarier it gets. Alone with your thoughts in pitch-black, unfamiliar terrain, you can only hope and pray you won't get left behind. This far from civilization, there was a distinct possibility that once hidden, you'd be lost forever.

In my case, there was no way I was going to venture more than twenty yards from the bonfire. I didn't want to run the risk of running into a pack of wolves, or worse still, a beast with two backs. Everyone knew the real allure of flashlight tag was getting to sneak private time for activities that would make even our disturbingly frank health teacher, Miss Scruggins, blush.

I waited for everyone else to scatter up the banks of the river and into the woods before I shuffled across the ice to wait out the game in Craig's Jeep. In his backseat, I burrowed under the flannel blanket he kept there for emergencies. It was scratchy and smelled alternately of men's cologne and wet dog.

Looking out the window, I could still see a few darting pinpricks of flashlights as people scampered farther into the brush until finally, the black woods swallowed them whole. Overhead, the Northern Lights warped across the night sky like a giant flashlight beamed into the universe's funhouse mirror. The green luminescence danced overhead in strange mutations, making me feel drunk even though I had only barely nursed my plastic cup of Sprite and cheap vodka.

Living in Anchorage, where mini-marts, mega-malls, Starbucks, and Taco Bells are as common as in any big city of the lower forty-eight, it's easy to forget how truly isolated Alaska is. Yet once you get even thirty minutes outside of the city, you start to remember that we're sort of stranded here on the edge of the world. Internet, e-mail, cell phones, and satellite TV can't change the fact that we're a savage frontier at heart. Our little pockets of civilization are dwarfed by beautiful-but-unforgiving mountains, glaciers, forests, and tundra. There are even people living here who wish we'd never joined the United States, who'd love nothing better than to secede from the union. Although I'd never known anything other than this rugged landscape, I often felt a sense of loneliness and isolation that I doubt residents of St. Louis or Dallas could ever understand. This was home, but there was a bleakness and foreboding atmosphere that made you cling more tightly to the people in your life.

I wondered whether my mom was home from work yet. Probably not, if there was a late-night screening. She'd always told me she had accepted the job at the theater to help us earn a little extra cash, but the payoff didn't seem to be worth the slow and steady disintegration of my parents' relationship. I guess I should have felt fortunate that they didn't shriek at each other every day the way some people's parents did. But I would have welcomed a shouting match in place of the complete and utter silence that pervaded their marriage. When they were both home at the same time (and that was becoming less and less frequent), they roamed our small, three-bedroom house in completely separate spheres, like those plastic balls that hamsters run around in outside of their cage. If they came within three feet of one another, it was only to hand off a crying Ollie or to shovel a spatula full of scrambled eggs onto the other person's plate. Conversation between Mom and Dad was monosyllabic, and while they still kept up the charade of retiring to the same bedroom at night, that wasn't enough to convince me they weren't toying with the idea of divorce.

I could see that the stress was getting to Dad, and as for Mom, when I did try to converse with her, she seemed dead inside. There was a time when I could confide in her about anything, but I couldn't remember the last time we'd had a real heart-to-heart. Of course there was Dad, too, but how could I talk to him about my terror that they might split up? I'd either be certain to cause him pain or, worse yet, hear my suspicions confirmed—which absolutely wouldn't work for my current strategy of living in denial. So instead, I plastered a smile on my face every night, told funny stories, helped out with Ollie as much as I could, and prayed that the inevitable didn't come to pass.

Everything happening at home certainly cast a harsh and clinical light on my high school crush. How in the hell did I know what love was if even my pushing-forty parents were clueless? Was falling in love *ever* worth the inevitable heartbreak?

In the distance, I heard the shriek of a male voice and the crack of what sounded like tree branches breaking. Was that laughter? At least someone was having a great time. Twenty minutes ago, I'd come just inches away from having a grand old time myself. I could have sworn that Craig had wanted to kiss me. I knew he was drunk, but hey—*in vino veritas*. Maybe that cheap liquor was acting as some sort of truth serum. It was foolish and degrading, I know, to be consorting with these drunken idiots out here in the middle of nowhere. This wasn't me. And yet, in that instant, as Craig's face ventured slowly toward mine, I couldn't help but think that one kiss would somehow be all it took to release him from the spell that was making him forget who he really was.

A sudden movement of the car jolted me out of my reverie. Someone had returned to the rendezvous point early and was now leaning against the Jeep. Nearby, I heard footsteps pacing on the gravel. Then I heard Beth's voice. She sounded out of breath, and spoke in a barely audible murmur.

"What's done is done, Craig. It was an accident. I'm just as freaked out about this as you are, so just get a grip!"

"I can't believe this is happening. Oh my god! What do we do now?"

"Nothing! Just pretend like everything's normal. It's the only way."

"Are you out of your mind?"

I crouched lower under my blanket. Every hair on my body was standing on end. Whatever Craig and Beth were arguing about, I didn't want to know. But to exit the car or let them know I was in the backseat now seemed monumentally unwise.

"You need to just chill out, Craig!"

"How can you say that? We're talking about a life here, and I'm responsible."

"I know, sweetie. We both are. But don't worry. We'll figure something out."

A life? Why was Craig so freaked out? My heart sickened at what I inferred: Beth was pregnant. Didn't Craig say she'd thrown up at school a few weeks ago? Morning sickness, of course! For a second, I myself felt a bit nauseous at the discovery of Craig and Beth's secret.

"What you need to do right now is calm down so we can figure out what to do," I heard Beth continue.

"What to do?" Craig said. "Don't you understand? This is the worst thing that's ever happened to me." He was right on that account. Fatherhood, I was certain, did not play into the highly orchestrated master plan that Craig's dad had mapped out for him. A baby would unalterably change his life. I swallowed hard to try to clear the lump that was forming in my throat.

"It was an accident, baby. Don't make this worse than it already is. We can't go back and change what happened. It's just got to be our little secret."

They were quiet for another ten seconds or so. I prayed that they didn't decide to get in the car. I didn't move a muscle. I could hear the scream of girls being chased back to home base, and their stampede put an abrupt end to the conversation, apart from one last hurried remark.

"My god, Craig, you're shaking. Let's get back to the fire. Pull yourself together! And don't breathe *a word* of this to *anyone!*"

My heart was pounding a mile a minute. I must have sat in the car for five minutes or so mulling over what I'd heard. As more groups of out-of-breath asylum-seekers returned from hiding, I quietly crept out of the car, making sure to exit on the far side so that no one would see me, and only barely closing the car door with a soft click. Ambling in a roundabout path back to the warmth of the bonfire, I found Craig staring blankly at the flames while Beth hugged him from behind, her cheek resting against his broad back.

"Hey Craig, looks like your third wheel made it back alive," said Brett Sanders, nodding in my direction as he took a swig from his beer can.

Craig glanced at me vacantly, then returned his gaze to the fire, which lit his face a shade of deep red.

Back up on the banks of the ravine, I saw the glare of five more flashlights heading toward us, looking almost like distant medieval torches weaving in and out among the birches. They'd all be back in from the game of tag, soon. Only it didn't seem much like childish fun and games anymore.

CHAPTER EIGHT

Nothing in His Life Became Him
Like the Leaving It

THE SCREECH OF THE INTERCOM cut through home-
room like a scythe, but the voice that coughed and cleared its
throat anxiously wasn't that of our perky senior class secretary
with her usual Monday morning announcements. Instead it
was a beleaguered Mr. Kirkpatrick, who had the unenviable
task of explaining that one of East Anchorage High's most
popular and well-loved students would never again cross its
threshold.

"It is with great sadness that I confirm the reports many of you
have been hearing," our guidance counselor announced, his voice
husky with emotion. "Your fellow student Duncan Shaw died in
a tragic accident over the weekend." He added that there would
be grief counselors on campus throughout the week, and, instead
of the usual Friday afternoon pep rally, a memorial service would
be held in the gym.

"My door is always open. . . . " he said, trailing off and leaving
a stunned silence in his wake. For several moments no one said a
word, then the quiet was broken as students leaned in toward each
other, speaking in hushed tones. I looked down at my desk in a
daze and was aware of nothing else for the next half-hour. I didn't
even remember hearing the bell or shuffling through the halls to
first period, though I must have done it.

Mr. Kirkpatrick hadn't provided us with any of the gory details about Duncan's death, but the cloud of rumors swirling around school did the job for him . . . and then some. In Anchorage, news of this sort traveled with a speed that belied the city's growing population. It was a given that by dusk on Sunday half the students knew—or thought they knew—what had happened. So far this morning, I'd heard speculation that he'd committed suicide, his body found a few hundred yards from the hunting shack hanging from a low tree limb with his own belt as a noose. I'd also heard that when he was discovered on Saturday afternoon, his face was barely discernible, having been gnawed off by some sort of wild animal. Some people were convinced he'd passed out and choked to death on his own vomit. Others swore he'd fallen down a ditch, broken his leg, and froze to death.

All weekend long I'd been trying to will myself to imagine that Duncan's disappearance on Friday night could be explained away. But the conversation I'd overheard between Craig and Beth that night continued to haunt me. I tried to recall, word for word, what they had said to one another, but the fuzzy memories flitted around my brain like drunken butterflies, just out of my grasp. At the time, I had so instantly jumped to the conclusion that Beth was pregnant that I didn't even consider that there might be another, more sinister interpretation. Now, everything I thought I'd heard while huddled in Craig's car made me fear the worst. When Duncan hadn't shown up at the bonfire after the raucous game of flashlight tag, the only one who'd shown any visible concern was his girlfriend, Tiffany. As the party began to break up, she queried one person after another and was met with shrugs and dismissive laughter until finally, hiccuping nervously, she approached Beth and Craig just as the three of us were climbing into his Jeep.

"Have you seen Duncan?"

"Shaw?" Beth said, shaking her head. "The last time I saw lover boy was *hours* ago. He was in the corner making out with some freshman. Don't know her name." This was generally in keeping with what I knew of Duncan's schizophrenic love life, so I thought nothing of it. Tiffany was still protesting when Beth slid, snakelike, into the passenger seat of the Jeep and slammed the door, forcing me to walk around to the other side of the car, where Craig leaned his seat forward to let me in.

The trip home was as silent and unsociable as the first leg of the journey had been. The only difference was that Beth's left hand stayed gripped on Craig's thigh throughout the drive and she ignored me completely until she got out to release me from the backseat. I couldn't help but think about the baby I imagined was growing inside her. Having a child at the age of eighteen would change her life forever, not to mention throw a giant wrench into her grand plans to be Prom Queen. Beth was manipulative as hell, but I was pretty sure she wouldn't have gotten pregnant on purpose if it meant forfeiting the crown. A weary sensation of relief washed over me when Craig finally pulled up to my house. Beth opened her door, and as I squeezed past her, she grabbed hold of my elbow, forcefully, and asked, "Hey, who tagged you?"

"What?" I asked. In the moonlight, her pristine white cheerleading jacket glowed ghost-like. Not wanting to lock eyes with hers, mine landed instead on a spot on her shoulder. A tiny red dot, a mere pinprick-sized blemish was visible on the white leather. Could it have been blood?

"Who. Tagged. You." Beth said, enunciating slowly. Why had she been so insistent?

"Um, some freshman." I wriggled free of her grasp. "They all look alike, don't they?" Flashing a nervous smile, I waved in the direction of the Jeep and headed for my front door, practically at a run.

Mrs. Kimball's tremulous voice finally broke my reverie.

"Class, please pass your quizzes to the front of the room."

I'd been too immersed in my own thoughts to realize that, possibly trying to keep some semblance of normalcy in the classroom, our physics teacher had passed out her usual Monday morning pop quiz. Lost in thought, I had missed the whole thing. That was when Leonard, who sat to my right, reached over and placed on my desk a sheet of paper with the answers circled in pencil and my name printed in block letters at the top. He'd obviously taken the quiz for me. I turned to thank him, but he looked the other way as if in embarrassment—for once not using the opportunity to assail me with his badly formulated compliments. I was grateful.

The rest of the day was obviously shot to hell as students gathered in little clusters, comforting each other in shock and disbelief. Others walked zombie-like from class to class with a perpetually pallid look on their faces. A collection of bouquets and stuffed animals was starting to amass outside the hockey rink, and Duncan's locker was plastered with taped-up notes of condolence. On some level, everyone seemed affected by what had happened, from the thespians to the stoners. And although a few people were milking the drama—sporting black armbands made of construction paper seemed a bit gratuitous, after all— the general outpouring of emotion was a testament to Duncan's equal-opportunity friendliness. In truth, he'd been the only one of Craig's friends who didn't make me feel like a complete waste of space when I was in his company.

Grief counselors bogarted several of the classrooms on the first floor, arranging the desks in circles, presumably for group therapy sessions. Must be a depressing job, I mused. What somber scenarios did they encounter during the other 364 days a year? A local news network anchor and her camerawoman sat whispering to one another in two of the plastic chairs lined up outside the principal's office.

The last thing I wanted to do was talk about my feelings, so after bailing on fourth period I headed for the darkroom where

I knew I could be alone. No teachers would be worried about truants today. I walked the hallway toward the art annex and when I was about to round the corner of a bank of lockers, two voices— ones I had recently become all too familiar with—stopped me in my tracks.

"I just can't deal with the . . . the *circus* right now." Craig must have been standing just around the corner. His voice was low, a loud whisper. "Half of them didn't even know him. Not really."

"Damn it, Craig, we've got bigger issues right now." Beth's response was shockingly abrupt. "They're going to be questioning everybody who was at the party."

"I still can't believe he fell! I mean, the look on his face. . . . It still feels like some bad dream I'm going to wake up from. We should just tell the truth. I mean, I wanted to call the cops that night!"

"No one could have known the ice was that thin! It wasn't our fault."

"I punched him!"

"You were provoked, damn it!"

"Those things he said about you. What he did to you. I just couldn't stand there and let the guy get away with it."

"Forget all that—"

"How can I, Beth? I'm going to *jail* for this!"

"But you were only protecting me, Craig—"

"When he grabbed for you . . . I almost thought he was going to pull you in with him. I . . . dammit, I actually thought for a second you'd be able to pull him out," he said, punctuating his words with a groan.

"Of course I tried, but he caught me off balance," she said. "There was *nothing* I could do—nothing either of us could do. But the only thing that's important now is that we get our stories straight. If anyone asks, we'll say we headed upriver toward the turnpike. We weren't there. *Nobody* was there."

"They say he was alive for hours out there, you know. . . . "

"Craig, we both saw him go in the freezing water. He was probably dead in under a minute."

"But Chief Towers said he died of exposure. His body was found on *land*," he said angrily. "What if he *wasn't* dead? What if we could have done something to save him?" There was a pause before Beth finally responded.

"But you can't save Duncan now. You can only hurt yourself."

As I listened with my eyes as wide as saucers I was practically in a state of shock. So it was true. Beth wasn't pregnant. They'd been freaking out that night because they both had something to do with Duncan's death! Instinct told me to turn on my heels and get out of there as fast as possible. My Converse All-Stars barely made a sound as I started to back away, but just then, Craig rounded the corner. Our eyes locked, and I'm quite certain he could detect the look of sheer horror on my face.

"What the hell are *you* doing here?" He glared at me.

"Craig, I'm sorry about Duncan. If you need someone to talk to. . . . " It was the only thing I could think to say without betraying everything I'd just overheard. I was standing far enough down the hall at this point that I hoped he didn't suspect I'd been eavesdropping. Craig paused and gazed at me intently.

"You should stay away from me, Skye," he said, before continuing down the hall. My knees felt shaky and I dropped my messenger bag to the floor, letting my shoulders and head sink along with it.

CHAPTER NINE

Present Fears Are Less
Than Horrible Imaginings

BY WEDNESDAY NIGHT all of the local media outlets were reporting ad nauseum the "official" details of Duncan's death. It was even briefly mentioned on CNN during a special report on the rise of alcohol consumption among teens. Apparently, although it hadn't been cited by the police, the prevailing wisdom was that Duncan must have downed one too many before stumbling out into the woods to his death.

Although I carefully avoided watching television or reading the paper during that time, it was pretty pointless, because that's all anyone seemed inclined to talk about, including my parents. They wanted to know how much I had to drink that night, how many drinks I thought were "too many," and all sorts of similarly embarrassing and frankly useless questions. I thought about telling them everything, but somehow the words just wouldn't come out. Besides, communication in my family wasn't a strong suit these days. In any case, it was obvious that my mom and dad sensed I was on edge. I couldn't blame them for speculating, but I wasn't about to give them the real reason for my anxiety: that I might very well be an accomplice to murder.

On Friday morning, news crews circled the gym like vultures, awaiting the memorial service scheduled for three o'clock that afternoon. Kaya and I were crouched inside the senior visual display window in the reception area outside Principal Schaeffer's office hanging the Yup'ik masks when Tiffany and her parents were ushered in by Dottie Hen, Schaeffer's plump and frazzled secretary.

"I'm afraid Principal Schaeffer isn't here at the moment," she explained breathlessly, "but he said that you should wait in his office."

"That's fine; we don't need to see him." Chief Towers had his hand on Tiffany's shoulder. "We just wanted to make sure that Tiffany wasn't penalized for her absences this week."

"No, certainly not," said Miss Hen. "We all know what a terrible ordeal this must be for your daughter. . . . "

I stole a glance at Tiffany and the poor girl did look truly miserable. Her face was pallid except for two bright spots on either cheek, and her brown eyes were red and puffy. Between that and the unusually somber black dress she was wearing, she definitely looked like a woman in mourning. All she needed was a veil to complete the picture. Were the widow's weeds really necessary? They'd only been an item for two weeks, max.

"Miss Kingston, hon?" Miss Hen interrupted my train of thought. Damn, had I been thinking aloud? But then she continued, "Why don't you walk Tiffany to her class?"

As she and I walked along the hallway, the echo of Tiffany's heels clattering against the linoleum was the only sound. Just as it was starting to feel really awkward, she broke the silence.

"Did you know Duncan?" she asked softly.

"Only superficially. We sort of moved in different circles."

"But you were there, right? I saw you with Beth and Craig."

I nodded, wondering where this was going.

"You know, he wasn't as drunk as everyone is saying," she said, pushing her thick auburn hair out of her eyes and looking me in the face as if to see my reaction. I didn't really know what to say, but I stopped walking and waited for her to finish.

"He *wasn't*," she said again. "And he wasn't cheating on me. I know what everyone thinks, but he wouldn't do that. Somebody *has* to know what really happened. There's more to this. There's got to be."

"Okay," I said, not sure how to respond.

"He was always honest. That's the one thing you could count on with Duncan." The word "honest" hung in the air as if it were Duncan himself staring me down, accusing me, haunting me. "He even told me when Beth made a pass at him."

"You think Beth would really do that?" I said, thinking, not for the first time since that night, that maybe Kristy had been telling the truth after all.

"Yeah, you're not *surprised* are you?" she said with a withering look. Maybe she was smarter than I'd given her credit for.

"Not exactly."

"Did she tell you about it?"

"No, but it's not like Beth and I are friends or anything . . . the opposite, actually." She started walking down the hall again and I followed.

"Even if you were, I doubt it would be something she'd want to advertise. . . ." She trailed off, but I sensed an unspoken question behind her words.

"Well, I'm really sorry about Duncan," I said lamely as we reached room 113, freshmen English. I wished I could tell her what I knew, but it was hazy, uncertain, and liable to drag me down just as Duncan had been pulled down into the icy current. My self-protective instincts kicked-in, and I walked away from the poor girl feeling as though I had betrayed her confidence. I proceeded back down the hallway feeling more alone than ever and with absolutely no one I could confide in. Not a soul.

When I got back to the office, Kaya and Tess were standing outside the display window whispering conspiratorially.

"Skye," Kaya said, waving me over.

"What's up?" I said, still distracted by my conversation with Tiffany.

"Mr. Tether just dropped this off for Schaeffer," she said, showing me the cell phone she'd been hiding behind her back.

"So?" I was in no mood for idle conversation.

"We overheard him tell Dottie that he confiscated it from your boyfriend," Tess added, as if that explained everything.

"From who?" (Though I knew exactly whom she meant.)

"Apparently your not-so-starving wannabe artist was penalized for unlawful texting during history," confirmed Kaya.

"What are you doing with it?"

"Hen left it on the counter in plain sight." Kaya giggled. "We couldn't resist snagging it."

"We thought you'd want to return it to him," Tess said proudly, handing me the phone.

"Um, right," I said, "good idea." I didn't want to seem totally goody-goody, and it would give me an excuse to talk to Craig, who'd been studiously avoiding me. Now I just had to figure out how to give it to him—a tricky proposition considering we weren't speaking.

• • •

I planned to ambush Craig as he headed from class to the gym for the memorial service. If he saw me coming, he would be sure to head in the other direction, so I'd have to plot our rendezvous with extreme caution. At the very least, I was hoping it would lead to some clarification on the situation. All through next period, I puzzled over what to say and composed endless imaginary scenarios for how things might play out. Unable to concentrate, I finally raised my hand and asked to be excused to use the restroom. When I walked in, Kristy and her friend Emily—a petite junior with dark hair, an upturned nose, and a perpetual pout—were already in the bathroom. They both wore their cheerleading uniforms and sported black armbands. Their makeup bags and beauty paraphernalia were perched precariously on the back of the sink and windowsill. Kristy was pulling Emily's hair into a tight ponytail on the back of her head.

"Skye, long time no see," Kristy muttered through the bobby pins in her mouth.

"Hey," I replied, watching her as she pulled the pins out and thrust them in her makeup bag. Just what I needed right now; a conversation with Kristy. I assumed from her tone she and Beth had probably made up already and that I was no longer her new favorite person.

"I see you made it home from the party okay."

"What do you mean?"

"Well, you were riding with Beth. I thought she might have chucked you out the car door at a convenient overpass, or at the very least tried to claw your eyes out." Okay. Clearly they were still frenemies.

"Any word from Duff?" I asked nonchalantly, changing the subject.

"He texted this morning," she said. "His parents called and told him about Duncan, and he's devastated that he can't be here right now."

"They were pretty good friends, right?"

"The best," she said. "Since kindergarten. Well, until Craig showed up, anyway. After Duff left, Craig stepped in and became Batman's new Robin."

I pulled out my comb and began running it through my hair, at the same time berating myself for primping. First of all, like Craig would even notice, and secondly, I had never been one to spend hours in front of the mirror trying to be the fairest of them all. It just wasn't my style.

"We're doing a dance routine in memory of Duncan at the memorial service," Emily said in a confiding tone.

"That's nice, I guess," I said, thinking it was actually kind of ridiculous, but whatever.

Startled, I noticed that Kristy was looking at me the way a tagger might eye a pristine brick wall. "You know," she paused and placed her forefinger against the side of her mouth, "you actually have a really decent complexion. You would look seriously fab with a little blush and some lipstick."

"And mascara. She could really use some mascara," said Emily.

"No way." I was emphatic. "You are *not* going to give me a makeover right now." In fact, the only time I'd ever even worn lipstick was for the party. Of course, Craig did almost kiss me that night. Unless I'd imagined the whole thing.

"No, crazy girl! We don't even begin to have time for that, but how about some lip gloss?" she said.

"Well. . . ." I couldn't believe I was actually considering being one of Kristy's Barbie dolls. Yet I was so preoccupied that I found myself nodding an absentminded assent. Oh well, maybe a few more minutes with her would give me some more information about what had happened at her family's hunting shack.

"Emily, move it!" Kristy said, motioning her away.

"Fine then, I'm outta here," Emily said as she flounced off, arms folded and her ponytail swinging angrily.

I dropped my messenger bag to the floor as Kristy pulled me over. She searched through her makeup bags carefully, lips pursed in thought, rejecting first one tube, then another.

"Let's try this one," she said finally, twisting open a tube of gloss. "Hold still."

"Okay," I said, trying not to move my lips as I perched in Emily's former spot on the edge of the porcelain sink.

"You know," Kristy said in a hushed tone, "Craig ought to look out."

"Huh?" I tried to keep still but gazed at her questioningly.

"Well, Duff's gone—practically banished—and now Duncan . . . dead." She pumped the lip-gloss wand back in its tube, giving me a chance to speak up.

"Yeah, so. What does that have to do with Craig?" I felt a cold dread travel up my spine.

"They have something in common. Beth's thrown herself at them all," she said with a shrug. "It's like a curse or something."

Now I was thoroughly confused. I thought back to what Tiffany had told me about Beth making a play for Duncan, and now Kristy was acting as if Duff was among her romantic targets, as well. None of this jibed with how possessive Beth was of Craig.

"You can't really think. . . ."

"I'm just saying," said Kristy, stepping back to admire her work. "It's too bad, that's all. And, of course, it gets Beth a little closer to what she wants." I hopped off the sink and turned to look at myself in the mirror, where our eyes met. "Convenient for her that Duff and Duncan are both out of the way. Now no one stands between her and Craig becoming Prom King and Queen." Then she smiled airily. "Aren't you going to get that?" she said.

That's when I noticed a buzzing coming from my messenger bag. I knew my phone was off, so it had to be Craig's.

"Here," she said, handing me my bag. "You never know, could be important." I didn't want to explain how and why I was in possession of Craig's phone, so I scrounged around until I found his cell and pulled it out. I immediately saw it was a text from Beth. Before I could stop myself, I clicked on the message:

WTF??? Suck it up. I don't have time for yr bullshit. Act normal and everything will be fine!!! Seriously, babe, be a man and f-ing GET IT TOGETHER or you will ruin everything.

I gasped and stuffed the phone back in my bag.

"What's up?" Kristy asked.

"Nothing," I said, hoping she wouldn't notice that my hands were shaking. "My mom just wants me to babysit after school." Kristy eyed me curiously but didn't say anything. I had to get out of there and go somewhere where I could think. "Thanks for the lip gloss," I said lamely and backed out of the bathroom.

How could I give the phone back to Craig after this? He'd surely know I read the message. It didn't help that he already suspected I might know something after our recent hallway run-in. Returning it to the principal's office now was out of the question—anyone might read it and put two and two together. Besides, who knew what other incriminating info was buried in his cell? This was all spiraling out of control so fast. What I needed more than anything was time. Time to think. Time to figure this out. In the meantime, I'd have to hide Craig's phone where no one would be able to find it.

Abandoning my plan to bump into Craig, I headed toward the gym with the rest of the students, but all I could think about was the text message. It was already burned into my brain as if I'd read it a hundred times instead of only once. As I squeezed into the gym, I was surprised to see what looked like chaos, rather than the respectful quiet I'd expected. Camera crews stood six or seven people deep on the far end of the gym, while Chief Towers and several police officers roamed the floor. Some of the cheerleaders were practicing their routine in a corner of the basketball court as parents and students looked on from the bleachers. I recognized the mayor, who stood at the podium talking with Principal Schaeffer and Mr. Kirkpatrick.

I headed up the stairs toward Jillian and Megan, who were on the fourth row of risers, but someone grabbed my arm and stopped me. I turned around to face Craig. His eyes had dark shadows under them, and I fought a strong urge to put my hand on his cheek.

"Skye," he said, still holding my arm. "I'm sorry about the other day."

"It's okay," I said, and then it was as if all the noise in the gym had been turned down like the way things sound when you plunge your head under water in the bathtub.

"How are you?" I said.

"Not fine. I don't know."

"This sounds annoyingly cliché, but still, I really meant what I said. If you ever, like, need anyone to talk to—" Just then I heard Jillian's voice in my ear.

"Skye! Earth to Skye. Didn't you hear me?" She handed me a camera and took my bookbag. "I need you to cover this. You can use my camera since you obviously didn't bring yours."

"But. . . ."

"No 'buts,' Skye, this has to go in the paper and, naturally, we need you to take the photos."

I looked at Craig, but he just shrugged his shoulders helplessly.

"So what are you waiting for?" Jillian said, pushing me gently toward the basketball court. "Start shooting."

A guttural harmonic drone echoed up into the rafters and sent a hush over the bleachers. A lone bagpiper's slow and sobering rendition of "Amazing Grace" led the procession of Duncan's parents and two younger sisters—who carried a pair of their brother's skates and his hockey stick. They placed them next to an easel stand displaying a poster-sized photo of Duncan. I fought back the urge to cry, but noticed plenty of people around me had lost it. Despite Jillian's directive, I felt uneasy about taking pictures, realizing it would be callous and intrusive. I placed the camera on the metal bench beside me and let my heavy heart join those around me, purposefully not scanning the crowd to see where Craig had gone. Wearing blinders seemed a better option at this moment. I tried willing myself to be as stoic as forged steel. Instead I felt like a piece of ceramic with a hairline crack, about to lose all of its structural integrity.

Three eulogies, one tactless cheerleader routine, and a moment of silence later, the memorial service was over. I found Jillian and traded her the camera for the return of my bag. The night air was bracingly cold, so I practically jogged over to the car, then sat shivering inside waiting for the windows to defrost. Would Craig ever confide in me about what really happened, and, if so, was I ready to hear it? The god's honest truth? No. I wondered if the goose bumps on my flesh were from the temperature or the instinctive fear that things were going to get worse before they got better.

When I arrived home, I went straight down the hall to my bedroom, locking the door behind me. I powered down Craig's cell, removing the SIM card. The only eyes that watched me as I wrapped the phone in an old T-shirt and hid it in the back of my closet were those of Jeff Buckley, who stared tragically down at me from the poster above my bed. I tossed the SIM card into the trashcan under my desk and tumbled onto my bed in exhaustion. Now I was going to put this whole incident behind me. In all probability, the best thing I could do would be to stay as far away as possible from Craig MacKenzie and Beth Morgan. Whether Kristy was joking or not, those two did seem to be cursed with bad luck. Why did I have to be caught up in all this? It seemed like I was never going to put it behind me, no matter how hard I tried.

CHAPTER TEN

Say, from Whence You Owe
This Strange Intelligence?

WITH MIDTERMS CLOSING IN and the college application deadline looming like a ruthless, ugly ogre, December had me clamped in a vise grip. The tension at home was ratcheting up, and with every spare moment my brain reeled with speculation and angst about Duncan's death. Was I an accessory to murder for keeping quiet about what I knew? And yet, what *did* I really know? Only that Craig and Beth were involved in it up to their necks. Even if I had any intention of ratting them out, what facts did I really possess? Besides, it was already too late; Duncan was dead and there was no changing that fact. If it *was* an accident, like they'd said outside the Jeep that fateful night, how could I put Craig through any more hell than he was already in?

Wrestling with my conscience, and searching for the loophole that would absolve me from any sense of moral or legal obligation to come forward, I sought refuge in my usual hiding place: behind my camera. I threw myself wholeheartedly into assignments for the newspaper, tearing through dozens of rolls of film for superfluous photo features around campus—any pretext would do.

"Skye, Principal Schaeffer was raving about your snowflake series last week," said Jillian at our Monday staff meeting. "Of course, that was *after* he gave the bird to our First Amendment rights."

73

"What do you mean?" asked Megan, swiveling on her office chair, a Bic pen keeping her wavy blonde tresses held together in a knot on top of her head.

"Oh," Jillian said with a sigh, "He kindly requested that we eighty-six any more articles about Duncan's accident. Or should I say so-called accident. Claims it's insensitive to the grieving family."

I thought Schaeffer might have a point. Like a bad supermarket tabloid, we'd been running the story into the ground for weeks, with nothing new or enlightening to say about the matter. Jillian didn't think so, of course.

"It sucks, too, because I'd just gotten a copy of the coroner's report from the fellas over at the *Daily News*," she continued. "You'll never believe what it says."

"What?" She had my full attention now.

"Well, we already know Duncan died of exposure on the riverbank after falling into the freezing water, right? But the autopsy shows that he had contusions on his face consistent with a violent assault, along with a busted lip that he incurred *before* he'd fallen through the ice."

Although Duncan's untimely end had been the only topic of discussion for days on end, I still felt queasy when it was mentioned, and the word "autopsy" wasn't helping.

"You mean. . . . ?" said Lenny, leaning forward in his chair.

"Mmm hmm," Jillian nodded as if it had been what she was thinking all along. "Foul play. Chief Towers is going to announce tomorrow morning that he's stepping up the investigation."

Sitting cross-legged on the floor of the newspaper office, I played with the frayed hem of my jeans and tried to look unfazed as I let this new revelation sink in.

"I wonder if that means they'll re-interview everyone who was at the party," Megan said. "Somebody's *got* to know something."

Lauren Baker, our resident music critic and DJ of her own weekly podcast, "Anchorage Air Radio," walked into the office and dropped her heavy nylon backpack near an empty computer.

"Are you guys talking about Duncan?" she asked. "It's just so crazy sad. To think that he was actually probably still alive until sometime Saturday morning."

"If they'd only known where to search for him they could have gotten to him in time," said Megan. "I can't imagine slowly freezing to death like that, all alone in the dark."

I felt my throat tighten and my eyes started to well with tears. I had to get out of here. NOW. I grabbed my bag and coat and made for the door with my head lowered.

As I rushed through the hallway and down the stairwell, footsteps echoed toward me from below. I took a deep breath and tried to compose myself.

"Miss Kingston!" a frail voice said. "I've been meaning to confabulate with you all week."

Whatever "confabulate" meant, the last person in the world I wanted to do it with was Mr. Kirkpatrick. He paused on the landing, making it impossible for me to pass by. I prayed that he was too nearsighted to tell I'd been crying. But wasn't it his job to listen? Maybe he was just the person I needed to talk to.

"I was hoping to schedule a meeting with you about your college applications." He smiled faintly. "I noticed you're only applying locally, and while your choices are fine, to be sure, I think you might consider some other options."

"Yeah, well," I stammered. "I'm not sure. . . ."

"If you're worried about tuition, I know of several scholarship opportunities for someone with your grade point average and curriculum," he kindly explained. If he only knew that college tuition was the least of my worries. "I've been saving some pamphlets for you from institutions with reputable photography programs. And let me think . . . you scored a 1560 on your SATs, is that right?"

It never occurred to me that Mr. Kirkpatrick even knew who I was among the hundreds of students at school. I'd never so much as exchanged two words with him before, beyond responding with an unexpressive "here," during study hall roll call. Who knew he actually had a mental dossier with my name on it? As he droned on about Pell Grants and campus tours, I started to formulate how I could broach the subject that was weighing on me. He seemed like he genuinely cared. Could I trust him?

"I'm so sorry, but I'm late for a meeting right now. Drop by my office on Thursday morning and we can discuss some of your options," he said, smoothing down his thinning combover as he continued up the stairs, taking two hurried steps at a time. Whether or not I would divulge my shocking confession became a moot point. Now you see him, now you don't.

• • •

While loading the dinner plates into the dishwasher, I managed to work myself into a red-alert panic about the likelihood of being called in to talk to the police. I'd somehow avoided the first round of interrogations that took place in Principal Schaeffer's office in the week following the accident. Students who'd attended the party had been called out of class to give statements to a trio of detectives that included Tiffany's dad, the chief of police. To my relief and semiconfusion, I was never summoned. Overlooked, no doubt, because I was a forgettable nonentity. School authorities didn't associate me with "that crowd." But now that they were stepping up the investigation, they'd leave no stone unturned, meaning I probably couldn't get away with hiding under my proverbial rock much longer—especially since the police chief's daughter knew I'd been there.

What I needed more than anything was a distraction, something that could quiet all the worrisome thoughts bouncing around in my brain—at least for a few hours. It suddenly dawned on me that I couldn't go on this way. I couldn't hold this secret inside anymore. It was too hard, and it wasn't fair. This was too big for me. It was time to stop hiding from the truth and turn to the one person who'd always been able (at least until lately) to make it better. I poked my head into the bathroom where Ollie was chuckling his pudgy little head off, slapping his little palms against three inches of tub water and sporting a beard of soapsuds.

"Look, Skye—baby Santa," said Dad, who was kneeling in front of the tub with his sleeves rolled up. He shot me a second glance, brow furrowed. "What's with the coat and car keys?"

"I thought I'd go hang with Mom while she waits for the last show to wrap up. I'll be home before eleven, I promise."

"Well," he said. "I guess you can't get into too much trouble with your mother. Just drive slowly out there. The side streets are still a little icy from last night's storm. And hey—bring back a tub of popcorn if there's any left."

Driving out of the subdivision, I rummaged through the armrest compartment and popped in the copy of Bob Dylan's *Blood on the Tracks* that Kaya had burned for me a few weeks ago. The skeletal trees in the neighborhood sported twinkly white lights, and evergreen wreaths graced a few of the neighbors' front doors. Two huge, illuminated plastic reindeer lit up the front yard at the end of the block, looking nothing like actual reindeer. I'd developed a true love/hate relationship with Christmas in recent years, but maybe it would be more fun now that Ollie could get into the Yuletide spirit. Sometimes I thought that his wide-eyed wonder at the simplest and stupidest of things was my one salvation from being completely jaded and cynical.

Before the defrost setting on the dashboard had officially completed its job, I did a clumsy but sufficient parallel parking job in front of the Regent. The neon-lit markee proclaimed in bold black letters that *Rear Window* was the featured movie. The ticket booth out front was closed up for the night. Walking through the entrance, you were engulfed in a vampy bordello vibe: black walls, dingy red carpet, and posters of old movies in garish gold Rococo frames. Behind the glass concession counter, a youngish guy with bleached hair was Windexing the outside of the popcorn machine. He must have been a relatively new hire, because I'd never seen him here before.

"Excuse me?" I said. He glanced over his right shoulder. His earlobes were pierced with black rubber and hung unnaturally long. "I'm looking for Patricia?"

"She only works on Thursdays and Fridays." He'd turned completely around at this point, and I saw that his nametag read "Mitchell M."

"No, I think she's working here tonight. Patricia Kingston?"

"Yeah, I know. Like I said—it's not her shift."

I instantly felt like I'd just been punched in the gut. The bright packaging of Raisinets and Skittles under the glass case started to blend before my eyes like a watercolor painting. Mindlessly, I started for the exit, but before I reached the door, I turned back.

"Hey, can I go ahead and get a ticket?"

"The movie started a half-hour ago—"

"Yeah, I know. I don't mind." I reached in my bag and pulled out my wallet, searching around for the ten-dollar bill I thought I still had on me. Mitchell M. must have felt sorry for me because he waved me off.

"It's fine. Just go on in." I headed for the theater entrance and up the stairs to the balcony. There was no one else in the upper level and maybe only half a dozen filmgoers down below. I grabbed a seat in the middle of the front row of the balcony.

A Hitchcock classic probably wasn't the best movie for my peace of mind, especially one about a guy who thinks he witnesses a murder, but where else was I going to go? Home, to tell Dad that his wife was up to god-knows-what when she'd claimed to be slaving away for her family? I don't think so. Where *was* she, anyway? If she had a class, she would have just said so. Instead, she lied, which could only mean that she was having some sort of torrid affair. *Sickening.* I felt stressed and overwhelmed to the breaking point. Here I was trying to tell the truth—an awful truth—and I run into Mom's own wall of lies! Why was I doomed to carry the burden of everyone else's dark secrets? No more. It was settled now: I was officially done with trying to do the right thing. From here on out, I was just going to worry about myself. When you bury your head in the sand, at least you don't get slapped in the face.

On screen, Grace Kelly wore pearls and a flouncy, full skirt. Her hair looked like spun gold. Of all the crazy genetic combinations in the world, some people get to be born looking like her, while the rest of us have to make do with frizzy red hair, size 10 feet, and a nose that's just a little too "Roman" for its own good.

I rifled through my bag for my phone and thought about leaving Mom a message telling her there was an emergency at home, just to freak her out. It would serve her right. Instead, I thrust it in my bag and tried to concentrate on the movie. How ironic that Jimmy Stewart actually *wants* to figure out what happened to his neighbor? Here I was thinking about shutting the blinds for good and pretending I hadn't seen—or should I say heard—anything.

I normally wouldn't have sat through all the final credits, but I was trying to postpone going home. Should I lie my way through a conversation with Dad—"Mom was thrilled to have the company . . . said she'd be home soon but not to wait up"—or do I tell him the truth? Was I the snitch or the conspirator?

I glanced at the clock on my cell. It was ten after eleven. I was already late for my curfew—no point racing home now. Maybe I'd get lucky and Dad would have been too exhausted to wait up for me, figuring I was "bonding" with Mom. If not, then it didn't matter what time I got in. Late was late. Busted was busted. The last person to mosey out of the theater, I decided to hit the ladies' room before I braved the cold. Mitchell M. was wet-mopping the floor behind the concession stand, whistling along to the easy listening music that was still being piped in. I started across the empty lobby toward the bathroom, but when I pushed open the door, something blocked my way. Through the crack in the door, a big plastic yellow trashcan rolled to the side and someone, a janitor I supposed, opened the door to let me in.

One look at her face and I almost shrieked.

"Beth!?"

She looked equally surprised to see me, and definitely not pleased. She was wearing charcoal gray Dickies, black cross-trainers, and a ratty black thermal T-shirt with hot pink hearts on it. A plastic spray bottle of cleaner hung from her belt loop and she held a roll of paper towels. My school's bitchy version of Grace Kelly was cleaning toilets. Not wanting to run away like a startled chicken, but also not wanting to be in her presence for any longer than I had to, I sidestepped my way to the sink for a cursory hand-washing, feeling every bit as awkward as she must have felt. A dollop of liquid soap fell onto the sink top as I washed my hands. I grabbed for a paper towel from the metal dispenser to wipe it up, not wanting to cause a further mess for her.

"Leave it, Skye," she said. I meekly tossed my towel into her garbage can and sidestepped back to the door. "Surprised to see me here?" She wiped her forehead with the back of her arm. This was one of those damned-no-matter-how-you-respond moments.

"Uh . . . a little," I said, grasping for any small talk that might make this moment less excruciating. "Your uncle owns this place, huh?"

"Yes, Uncle Rodney and his noblesse oblige. He pays me minimum wage to clean up after people's disgusting messes here once the theater's closed."

"Oh."

"I'm lucky if I get out of here by one a.m. most nights. Not that I could sleep, anyway."

I didn't know what to say to this. Part of me pitied her. No wonder she was so unpleasant to be around—she was exhausted. Then again, her "this is so beneath me" lament seemed a little more dramatic than necessary.

"What about weekends?" I said. The job certainly hadn't hampered her Friday-night social life, after all.

"I come in the morning on Saturday and Sunday before we open," she said, her tone dull. I nodded casually, trying to act like it was no big thing.

"Well, I guess I'll see you tomorrow." Beth looked defeated as she rolled the garbage can away from the door again.

"For the record," she said, "people at school really don't know about me working here. I'd appreciate if you'd keep it that way." Typically, her request came across more like a command than anything. Little did she know that I was already protecting her from a whole lot more than her stupid rep. In any case, I'd had a shitty day and wasn't about to reassure her that her secret was safe with me. Lucky for her, I'd already checked out. People's problems were their own—not mine.

"Have a good night," I said enigmatically, and headed back toward the lobby.

CHAPTER ELEVEN

To Throw Away the Dearest Thing He Ow'd, As 't Were a Careless Trifle

LEONARD'S ABSURD COME-ONS were starting to look pretty good right about now. I peered deep into my shallow locker pretending to look for something that wasn't there while Brett Sanders leaned caddishly on the locker next to mine, invading my personal space.

"So, Red, I'm digging the gams today, among other things," he said, eyeing my legs, which were clad in black knit tights under a short khaki skirt. I didn't think it was too daring when I'd put it on this morning, but apparently, it had stoked Brett's legendary libido.

"Hmm, thanks," I said, still trying to appear preoccupied. He was wearing a voluminous crocheted Rastafarian hat—so entirely suited for a rich white kid near the Arctic Circle. It took every ounce of restraint not to pluck the dumb thing from his head and toss it in the nearby recycling container. His Bob Marley T-shirt, hemp necklace, and Salvation Army fatigue pants advertised his membership in the 4:20 crowd. Maybe that was the reason he was acting like such an idiot. I have no earthly idea why, but the guy had taken a sudden interest in me in the past week or so and was threatening to become a full-on barnacle.

"Dang, girl. What are you, five-nine, five-ten?"

"Something like that," I said.

Craig turned the corner and strode down the hallway in our direction. A welcome distraction—hopefully he could save me. He paused in his tracks when Brett flagged him down.

"Hey, Mac," Brett said. "I was just telling your little buddy here what a hottie she's turned into this year." He was?

"Whatever, Sanders." Craig was visibly annoyed. He sported a gruesome, greenish-purple black eye—a battle scar from his last hockey game.

"I'll give you credit for spotting her potential before the rest of us," Brett said, with a rakish leer in my direction, "but if you don't mind, I'd like a crack at it now."

Crack at it? What a pig.

"Knock it off, dipshit," said Craig. "Why don't you go find some tree to hump?"

"I *did*—a redwood, in fact." Brett winked at me, before sauntering away.

I expected that Craig would apologize on behalf of his asshole teammate, but instead, he turned to me and practically snarled.

"What the hell do you think you're doing?"

"*Me?*" I said, baffled. "What are you talking about?"

"Things were cool with us, before, but now you're getting all up in my business. Wanting to hang out with my friends, apparently *throwing* yourself at my friends, now. . . ."

"Whoa, whoa," I said. "Like hell I have! I think you're confusing me with someone else." He ignored this last remark.

"Yeah, well, if you're trying to win some kind of popularity contest, you've got a long way to go, and I'd appreciate it if you stopped using me to do it."

"Try giving that advice to the person who really needs it: your psycho bitch girlfriend!" I couldn't believe that just spilled out of my mouth. I slammed my locker door shut. Craig had obviously never seen me this riled up because I don't think I'd ever been this riled up.

"Look," he said. "You and I were friends once, I get it. But we're both in different circles right now."

"Funny you should say that because I'm the same person I've always been. You're the same person, too, underneath all this 'big man on campus' bullshit. Maybe we haven't been officially, publicly 'friends,' but I'm probably the one person in this school that really knows you and really cares about you, for that matter. From what I see these days, you could use a friend like that."

He stared at the floor, his arms crossed defensively in front of him.

After a pause, he said, "I just think it would be better for both of us if we kept our distance from now on."

"Hey, fine with me," I said. "You never know your friends from your enemies until the ice breaks. Right?"

Craig stared at me, searchingly. I saw fear in his eyes. How do you like your Beanpole now?

Before I had the chance to storm away in dramatic "FU" fashion, Principal Schaeffer rounded the corner, shoulder-to-shoulder with Tiffany's dad and two other official looking authority figures, striding purposefully like Mafia dons.

"Mr. MacKenzie," said Mr. Schaeffer, grabbing Craig by the scruff of his collar. "We'll be needing to talk to you again." So it was official. The investigation was stepping up, just as Jillian had foretold. Principal Schaeffer eyed me. "Miss Kingston . . . why don't you follow us to my office, as well."

My bladder surged in a panic. This was it. I swallowed hard, shut my locker door, and without a word accompanied them down the hall.

CHAPTER TWELVE

Look Like the Innocent Flower, but Be the Serpent Under It

DOTTIE HEN, SCHAEFFER'S GAL FRIDAY, gave me a reassuring smile as I sat in one of the chairs facing her desk.

"Kiss?" She pointed to a Christmas-tree-shaped glass container filled with red-, green-, and gold-foiled chocolates and shrink-wrapped candy canes.

I shook my head no thanks and she resumed her typing. Her half-moon reading glasses perched on the end of her nose like they were suicidal, weighing the pros and cons of jumping off into the void.

Craig had been sequestered with the cops for at least twenty-five minutes, if my sense of timing was at all accurate. I couldn't hear a word—only the clacking of Miss Hen's computer keys and her occasional "hmms" and "ahhhs" as she scrutinized her monitor.

I stared blankly out the window that overlooked the school parking lot, waiting . . . paralyzed with fear. It would be futile to concoct a story. I was a crappy liar. Besides, I had no idea what the police might already know. Maybe there was someone else at the party who knew even more than I did, who'd ratted all of us out. Why else would I be sitting here? Maybe Craig would confess, and I wouldn't even have to be called in at all. Yeah, he'd been an asshole to me minutes ago, but the thought of seeing him hauled away to juvie in a squad car caused a giant, painful lump to form in the back of my throat. Soon, I'd have to decide my fate—and possibly Craig's. The moment of truth. Or was it? I wasn't even there when Duncan died, after all. What I knew, or *thought* I knew about that night hinged on a few half-mumbled snippets of conversation I was unlucky enough to have overheard; the very definition of hearsay. I pictured myself weeks or months from now, sitting not outside Principal Schaeffer's office but on the witness stand, a throng of journalists and cameras crammed along the perimeters of the courtroom as some imposing lawyer forced me to give the evidence that would damn Craig forever. The idea put me in a panic. Maybe it was the right thing to do for Duncan and his family. But then, why was it only making me feel more confused and frightened than ever? What was the expression? "The truth will set you free?" Easy for me to say—I wasn't the one who'd be going to prison. At least, I certainly hoped not. Perhaps the fact that I'd said nothing so far made me somehow complicit! I heard the sound of chair legs scraping on the floor on the other side of the door and knew I had only seconds, now, to decide what I was going to do. In a last-minute mental whirlwind, I finally resolved to tell the truth, the whole truth, and nothing but—*only* if they asked. I wouldn't lie, but I wouldn't volunteer any information, either. The chips would have to fall where they landed . . . come what may.

The door to Mr. Schaeffer's office opened and Craig walked out. He didn't so much as glance at me as he exited. Miss Hen's phone rang once. She picked it up, listened for a moment, then looked at me.

"They're ready for you now, hon," she said, sympathy in her voice.

I'd never been in the principal's office before. For some reason I'd expected expensive walnut furniture and a high-backed leather desk chair—an antique globe in the corner, perhaps. Instead, I walked into a messy, fluorescent-lit room with steel filing cabinets, a faded, decades-old poster of Bill Cosby that said "READ!" on one wall, and dusty Venetian blinds with several bent slats. Nowhere near as executive-looking as I'd expected.

Everyone in the room was standing except for Chief Towers, who was sitting behind Schaeffer's desk. Heavyset with his arms crossed, he gestured with his head toward the empty chair facing him. I took a seat. No one introduced the other two guys, but I could only assume they were detectives, too. My heart was pounding like a bad techno song, and my skin felt suddenly wet and clammy.

"Skye," said Principal Schaeffer, who was looming behind the chief. "Let me reassure you that you're not in any trouble. You're a good girl, one of our most responsible students, and you needn't be alarmed—"

Chief Towers raised his arm to silence him.

"Miss Kingston," he said, his tone gruff. "Although this is not a formal questioning, I need to inform you for the record that we are tape-recording this conversation. You are under no obligations to answer our questions without a lawyer and/or your parents present, but as I've stated, this is not a formal deposition. As your principal explained, you are not in any kind of trouble, we're just trying to clarify a few things. Do you understand, and can we count on you to cooperate with our investigation?" I nodded and whispered my assent.

"Good," he said. "Now, we've been led to understand that you were in attendance at the party which was held on Friday, November tenth, at the Winters's hunting shack. Is that correct?"

I nodded in the affirmative. My hands were trembling so I clenched them and grasped the bottom of my skirt.

"Miss Kingston, you'll need to answer vocally, with a yes or no, so the tape recorder can pick it up."

"Okay," I said, feeling sheepish. "Yes."

"Had you ever been to this property before?"

"No."

"Did you see Duncan Shaw at the party?"

"Yes." I looked at the ceiling, half expecting to see some harsh interrogation light shining down on me. But these were all yes-or-no questions. Maybe I could make it through this unscathed.

"Did you speak with him that night?"

"No."

"From what you saw of him, was there anything that struck you as unusual?"

"What do you mean?"

"Meaning, did he seem like himself? Did he look upset or angry at all?"

"I only saw him for a second," I said, carefully minding my words. "He seemed fine." The chief scrawled something illegible from my perspective on his yellow legal pad. What was he writing? It was strange to think that Tiffany Towers probably had this man wrapped around her little finger at home. He seemed like Godzilla to me.

"What time was it when you actually saw Duncan?"

"I'm not sure . . . maybe eleven-ish."

"And were you drinking alcohol?" My face turned red and I glanced at Principal Schaeffer, horrified. Would answering truthfully lead to my expulsion? He offered back a compassionate look.

"It's okay, Skye . . . you can be honest." I brushed my hair back off my face with a still-quavering hand.

"I had a little."

"And how much do you consider 'a little'?"

"One shot and a few sips of vodka. That's all." I was so ashamed of myself. I wanted to melt into the floor.

"Would you have described yourself as drunk?"

"No."

"Did you see Duncan get into an altercation with anyone at the party?"

"No."

"Now, when the game of flashlight tag got underway that night, who were you with?"

"Pardon me?" I glanced up from the desk, confused.

"Did you partner up with anyone?"

"No. I was by myself."

"By yourself?"

"I didn't participate. I stayed behind."

"Were you the only one who stayed behind?"

"Yes, I think so."

"So you weren't with any of the others?"

"Yeah . . . I mean, no."

Chief Towers stood up from the chair, leaning onto his palms, which were planted firmly on the desk. He was looming over me now, but still looking at his notes.

"Did you see who Duncan might have left the property with?"

"No," I answered. "Tiffany, I guess."

"I *did not ask* you to guess, only to answer my questions!" My stomach started doing somersaults. "What did you do while the others were gone?"

"Nothing. I waited for them to come back."

"And how long did it take before people came back?"

"Maybe twenty minutes. Maybe a little longer."

"Who returned first?"

Oh god, here's where it got dicey. If I answered that Craig and Beth were the first ones back, I might be contradicting their testimony. If they wanted to position themselves far away from Duncan's whereabouts, they might have changed this detail of the story.

"Miss Kingston, I'll ask it again. Did you see who was the first to return to the property?"

In his phrasing of the question, I discovered my out. Seeing was different than hearing, was it not? I'd *heard* Craig and Beth, but I didn't *see* them until they were amongst the others at the campfire. Here goes . . .

"No, I didn't see the first people back. I was trying to stay warm in a car and when I got back to the bonfire, there were already about a dozen people there."

"At the bonfire—no one said anything about Duncan?"

"No," I answered truthfully.

"Nothing whatsoever?"

"It was only later, when Tiffany started freaking out."

"And what was the response to that?"

I paused before answering truthfully again, with as much tact as I could muster. "People joked that Duncan was probably just trying to give Tiffany the slip." I cringed inwardly. "He had a history of going MIA on his past girlfriends, so no one seemed worried." Chief Towers flushed.

"And you, Miss Kingston? What did *you* think?" Oh shit. I tried to answer truthfully again without actually divulging any pertinent information, though the only thing I could think of was the tiny spot of blood I'd seen on Beth's jacket when they dropped me off that night.

"I don't really hang out with this crowd normally, so I didn't know quite what to think." It was true, to a degree, but it wasn't the *god's honest* truth. The sentence came out involuntarily, as if I were lip-synching the words while someone else spoke. Chief Towers, still leaning on the desk, stared at me with penetrating eyes, as if he was not entirely satisfied with this last remark. The longer he fixed his eyes at me, the more I started to crumble inside. He obviously knew there was something I wasn't saying. Should I just end the nightmare now and come clean with what I knew before I sunk into this quagmire any deeper? Might it not come as some twisted sense of relief to be called on my hair-splitting bullshit and have the truth come tumbling out for the whole world to hear? I knew I couldn't keep up this charade, so it would be better that things ended here and now, once and for all. Just as I was about to relent and tell everything, Principal Schaeffer stepped forward and whispered something in the chief's ear. The burly cop looked dubious, but Schaeffer nodded once more, as if to corroborate what I'd just said.

"I think Miss Kingston has learned a very tragic lesson about hanging out with the wrong crowd, isn't that right, Skye?" said Schaeffer. I cleared my throat but said nothing, stunned that the conversation had just taken this tamer turn. I held my breath and hoped that this was almost over.

Chief Towers flipped through a few more pages on his clipboard and gave me a grim glance, as if I'd just completely wasted his time.

"Well, I suppose that will be all, then," he said.

"Thank you very much, Skye," said Principal Schaeffer. "Please return to your sixth-period class. Miss Hen will write a note excusing your absence."

"That's it?" I said, confused. "You're finished with me?"

"Thank you for your assistance."

Was that it? Did I just run the gauntlet unharmed? I breathed in deeply, grabbed my messenger bag, and walked numbly out of the office, only to momentarily freeze on the other side of the door. Beth was in the same chair in the reception area where I'd been seated before. Why did she always elicit the same startled reaction from me? As I waited for Miss Hen to fill out my absentee form, I glanced at Beth again out of the corner of my eye. She was clutching the oversized designer purse she used for a book bag against her torso with both arms. Her legs were crossed and her left ankle boot tapped the air in a nervous, impatient twitch.

"You can go in now, Beth," said Miss Hen, reaching up to hand me my pass. As Beth slid by me, I wished, for one second, that I could telepathically tell her not to be frightened and that everything would be okay. But, really, why should I tell her that? She was the cause of this whole thing! Accident or not, she knew the truth about Duncan's death, and maybe if it all came to light, I could stop feeling so twisted up in my gut every night before I fell asleep. Besides, now that Craig was being such a jerk to me, I was getting mighty close to not caring whether he ended up in trouble anyway. Hiding Craig's cell was the last thing I would do to save his butt, and he would never even know I did it. Why did I care what happened to some cute boy who once deigned to give me the time of day? He wasn't my problem anymore, and Beth shouldn't be, either. The police had no reason to involve me any further in their investigation now that I'd navigated their murky line of questioning with my conscience intact. Things were going to be okay after all, at least where I was concerned. And someday, sooner or later, the nagging feeling in the back of my brain would take up residence somewhere else. It just had to.

CHAPTER THIRTEEN

I Have Almost Forgot
the Taste of Fears

IF YOU ASK ME, there's something creepy about a talking doll, but my baby brother was officially enraptured with Tickle Me Elmo. He sat on our living room floor for the better part of Christmas morning, heaving uncontrollable belly laughs at the red Muppet's giggling antics. I knew I was going to have to find a way to deactivate Elmo's battery after a few more hours of this, but in the meantime, I, too, was cracking up watching Ollie shriek and bounce and clap his hands as if he had never in his short life seen anything so hilarious. Perhaps he hadn't.

My mom padded from the kitchen back into the living room in her candy-cane covered flannel peejays, her ceramic "Trust me, I'm a med student" mug newly refilled with coffee. She handed the cup good-naturedly over to Dad, who was sitting on the sofa. Then she plopped down on the couch and nestled right up against him. What in the hell was going on with these two? This overt cuddling was not like them, at least, not in my recent memory. I turned my head from them, not wanting to make them feel self-conscious lest I ruin the moment.

They seemed atypically happy with each other in the last few days, out of nowhere rocking a Norman Rockwell vibe. Mom's college classes were suspended until after the winter break, so she was home more, and she'd even baked a pecan pie, which came out a little soggy, but still. I couldn't account for the sudden turnaround. I'd never spoken to her about the night I'd discovered her *not* working at the Regent, but now, maybe it was a moot point.

I would have investigated their newfound reconnection a little further were I not so distracted by the laptop I had unwrapped earlier this morning from "Santa."

"Dad installed Photoshop on it for you," Mom said, winking at me.

"Well, I know my young Skye-walker still uses film," Dad said, "but I figured maybe it would come in handy for you at some point. We can look for a sale on a scanner/printer in the Sunday circulars and find a good deal."

"Thanks, Dad. I love it."

"It's only a used one. But it's not too old, and a buddy of mine from work loaded it up with software."

"It'll be great for you to take with you to school next year," Mom said.

"Oh, hey, about that," I said, perking up even more, "I've applied for a couple of scholarships that the guidance counselor at school thinks I've got a shot at. I mean, I'm not getting my hopes up or anything, but you never know."

I'd officially completed all my college applications and submitted them well before the deadline, even managing to write what I thought was a pretty decent personal essay despite everything that was weighing on me these last few weeks. I was finally starting to feel like I could breathe again having gotten that off my plate. Now, the waiting game.

"Once the flood of acceptance letters start rolling in we can sit down and figure out the finances," said Dad, who glanced at my mom and beamed. "If we can send one Kingston beauty to college, we can send two, right?"

Mom reached over and tousled his hair, which was only just beginning to gray around the temples.

"That reminds me, Knick-Knack-Patty-Whack," he said, fiddling with a puzzle of interlocking chains that had been one of his stocking-stuffers. "Tomorrow's Tuesday. Back to the grindstone—or should I say, ticket booth—for you."

I looked up from checking out my different screensaver options and watched for Mom's reaction. She bit her lower lip.

"Actually, I've been meaning to tell you. Rodney had to cut my hours. I'm down to just Thursdays and Fridays now. With all the studying I'm having to do for school, it seemed like it was for the best. Besides," she said with a grin, "I'm looking forward to spending some more evenings at home with my family!"

I glanced back down at my laptop, not sure what to think. Was she lying now, or telling the truth? Maybe this was the completely innocent explanation for why she wasn't at the Regent the night I dropped in. But wouldn't she have been at home if that were the case? It was also possible that I was right all along about her having an affair, and she'd only just decided to end it. Regardless, she appeared to be trying to turn over a new leaf with regard to Dad and us. In typical ignorance-is-bliss fashion, I decided it was no longer worth worrying about. Everything in my life was looking up, and that sort of good news deserved a fitting tribute.

"Who wants pancakes!?!" I said, closing my laptop and jumping to my feet.

"Kye! Pantake!" answered Ollie, adorably.

"Chocolate chips in mine, please!" Mom said, getting up to join me. As we shuffled through the detritus of giftwrap and entered the kitchen, I could still hear Elmo erupting into spasmodic fits of glee in the living room. Maybe I wasn't quite so demonstrative, but in a weird way, I could kind of relate to the little guy.

• • •

Early the next evening, we packed up the plethora of baby gear associated with taking Ollie out of the house. Stroller? Check. Diaper bag? Check. Plastic baggies full of Cheerios? Moist towelettes? Enough small toys for his baby-sized attention span? Check, check, and check. It felt like gearing up for a military invasion, but in reality, we were only headed downtown to see the Crystal Gallery of Ice. Every year, international teams using chainsaws and pick-axes spent forty-eight hours creating some of the most brilliant sculptures imaginable in the town square. The event always drew large crowds, and it was coolest to see after dark when the sculptures, backlit by lights, had a beautiful incandescence.

Mom and Dad were still in an exceptionally good mood as we pulled into a public parking lot and began to extricate my brother and his gear from the car. While waiting for them to get the stroller set up, I checked out my reflection in the car window. I couldn't decide if my green hunter's cap with its earflaps and lamb's wool lining was funky-cool or just plain dorky. Still, the color contrasted nicely with my flame-red tresses, which for once hung in a nice subtle wave without too much unruly kink or frizz. All in all, I thought I was looking damn cute.

"Hey, I'm gonna wander," I said. I had my camera and couldn't wait to start getting shots of the ice sculptures and the crowd, both of which were sure to fascinate.

"Skye, honey . . . we just got here!"

"Aw, let her go, Patty," said my dad. "If we don't bump into you in forty-five minutes, call us on Mom's cell so we can meet up."

"Okay, I will," I said, simultaneously snapping a picture of them. "Have fun you kids!"

"Right back atchya."

I padded across the packed snow to check out the sculptures. From where I stood, I could see replicas of the Sphinx, a giant ice castle, a stegosaurus the size of a VW bus, and a true-to-life ice rendering of all four Beatles. The detail on each sculpture was worth marveling at, but I was more in awe of the slick, glassy surfaces and the way they refracted the light so beautifully. Viewed in this sparkling wonderland, ice seemed incredibly regal, on par with gold or precious gems. And yet it was only water, which drop by drop was melting away. In a matter of days, at most, these astonishing works of art would vanish. Why did things always have to feel so fleeting? Sometimes I wished I could go through life carrying a remote control, one that would let me pause on the good times, like yesterday morning, for example, or let me fast-forward through all the crappy business in between. They say time flies when you're having fun, but boy does it move at a snail's pace when you're worried or depressed or anxious.

Wandering around the festival, I experimented with taking some pictures out of focus, thinking the array of colored lights mixed with the movement of the crowd might result in something impressionistically abstract. The chipper sound of Christmas carols mingled with the harsh buzzing of chainsaws that some of the sculptors still wielded. That, along with the smell of fried dough and popcorn, resulted in an environment of sensory overload. I had to keep reminding myself to look up from my camera's viewfinder at intervals so I didn't get dizzy. As tall as I was, I couldn't help but wish for a stepladder or high perch from which to take a more panoramic shot of the white-and-silver wonderland.

I instantly recognized the next sculpture I came across. It was a perfect replica of Auguste Rodin's *The Kiss*. This was passion personified: two lovers locked in a fervent embrace. I peered through my camera's viewfinder and adjusted the lens. The man's right hand was tenderly placed on the woman's left thigh. Her arm was flung desperately around his neck, and their faces pressed close to one another. They weren't wearing a stitch of clothing, and yet, this sculpture didn't say "lust"—not to me, at least. There was something so pure, idealistic, and uncalculated about the image. You didn't have to be in love to understand the magnitude of love when you looked at it.

"If I ever had a kiss like that one, I don't think I'd mind being frozen in that position for all eternity," I heard someone to my right say. As I lowered my camera, my stomach went topsy-turvy. I knew the voice. Turning to see him standing inches away from me, looking too hot for words, only made my stomach queasier for some reason.

"I thought we were avoiding each other these days, to prevent me from making any further claims on your popularity."

"You know that's not what I meant. I'll admit I was out of line, but just know that I was going through some stuff."

"Stuff, meaning being hauled in to talk to the chief of police again?"

He paused for a moment before replying, as if weighing his words carefully. "Stuff at home. You wouldn't understand."

"You'd be surprised." With my head lowered, I dug the toe of my boot into the snow, making a divot.

"Speaking of the chief of police, I hope you weren't too freaked out," he finally said. "Was it awful?"

"You ask that *now*?" I shook my head in disbelief. "You saw that I was going to be fed to the lions in Schaeffer's office, and you only think to ask me about it two weeks later? Gee, thanks for the belated concern, but you know what? You were right to end our sham of a friendship that day. Your troubles aren't mine anymore."

"What's that supposed to mean?" he asked, searching my face for an answer. His eyes looked weary. When I didn't respond, Craig ran the palm of his hand across his face, as if in physical pain, and walked away.

I meant what I had said to him. I was relieved not to have to worry about whether he'd be doing the perp walk while the rest of us walked the stage at graduation. I was sick of analyzing his dysfunctional relationship with Beth and holding my breath every time he got slammed against the boards in a hockey game. I was here-and-now officially declaring my brain to be a Craig-free zone. Still, I wondered what he was getting at when he said he had some problems at home. Having recently been through "stuff at home" myself, I could relate. Problems with his dad, no doubt. The guy was always ragging on Craig for the smallest things. I remembered on one particular occasion when I'd first met Craig, Mr. MacKenzie had blasted him about needing a haircut. "My only son, walking around looking like a woman," he ranted for the entire week, even after Craig had gotten it trimmed shorter.

"This from a man who parades around in a plaid kilt and knee socks every St. Andrew's Day," Craig had laughingly confided to me at the time. I don't think he was afraid of his dad so much as he was desperate to please the man. I gathered that the more dutifully he obliged the old man's wishes, the more his dad tried to control him and dictate his future. Come to think of it, Mr. MacKenzie and Beth Morgan had more than a few things in common.

So whatever. If he was having more problems with his dad, that was too bad, but in my new Craig-free zone, this was not my concern. You heard me right. Skye Kingston was taking the imaginary remote control of life and hitting the "delete" button on one Craig MacKenzie. And what did he mean by that "I-wouldn't-mind-kissing-like-that-for-all-eternity" business, anyway?

CHAPTER FOURTEEN

Out, Damned Spot!

VALENTINE'S DAY. The most ridiculous Hallmark excuse for a holiday ever. End of story. You're either totally guilted into buying crappy gifts and schmaltzy cards for someone, or, in my case, being made to feel like a pathetic loser who will go to her grave alone and unwanted. Isn't being in love reward enough without needing a special day as a bonus? Why isn't there a holiday for all the sad sacks of the world who might actually need a crappy gift or schmaltzy card to cheer them up? I'm waiting for the "Let's All Mope!" day or a "Life Sucks" three-day weekend. Aren't we the ones who really need that box of chocolate?

I scanned the classroom noting the giddy excitement of several of my female classmates. Their eyes were locked feverishly on the sophomore girl who, clad in a pink velour track suit, inched between the rows of desks, delivering long-stemmed roses one at a time. Wavering between fear, anticipation, and abject longing, each girl clearly hoped a boyfriend or secret admirer had ponied up the two dollars necessary to send a rose to his beloved. Some girls would receive multiple roses, others none at all. Oh, the humanity.

Surprisingly, the only person who looked like she cared even less than I did was Beth. She was staring out the window, semi-catatonic, her face an unreadable canvas. Probably imagining her and Craig's future coronation as Prom King and Queen, I thought dismissively. Not that it mattered to me . . . Craig MacKenzie, after all, was the furthest thing from *my* mind.

Rolling my eyes, I looked back down at my battered copy of the *Oxford Anthology*, rereading the Shakespearean sonnet we'd been discussing before the rude interruption of Cupid's Pepto Bismol–tinged messenger. I doubted that we'd get back to it since everyone was chattering and distracted, and there were only a few minutes left before class was dismissed.

My mistress' eyes are nothing like the sun;

Coral is far more red than her lips' red;

If snow be white, why then her breasts are dun;

If hairs be wired, black wires grow on her head. . . .

Based on that description, his mistress would never have managed a prom date at this school. The concept of inner beauty doesn't exactly fly here. Lost in thought, I hadn't noticed right away that Beth was standing over me. I looked up to see her practically boring holes in my skull with her glowering eyes, a look of unmistakable hatred on her face.

"Is this your idea of a joke?" she said in an angry voice as she brandished a rose, waving it in front of my face.

"What are you talking about?"

"This!" She yanked off a cardboard tag tied to the stem by a red ribbon and shoved it under my face. Trying to remain calm, I opened the tiny, folded card and read the typed note on the inside: *You never really know your friends from your enemies until the ice breaks.*

"You said the same thing to Craig—he told me about it. What are you trying to imply, anyway?"

"I don't know what you're talking about," I said, although I did remember using the line when Craig had banished me from his friend roster. Oh no, she thinks it's about Duncan, I thought. "This isn't from me."

Just then the bell rang, so I scooped up my books and made a mad dash for the door. "You should talk to Kristy," I threw out over my shoulder. I didn't want to completely rat out her former best friend—I clearly wasn't in the business of narcing—but wasn't going to stand around and take all the heat for this little stunt, either.

My hands were shaking as I fumbled with my locker combination. Clearly Beth still suspected that I knew something linking her and Craig to Duncan's death. Since Christmas I'd convinced myself that I had just been paranoid about the whole thing. True, memories from that night still rose to the surface every so often, but for the most part, I'd kept those thoughts at bay as I focused on my photography, my college applications, and the fact that my family life was finally on an even keel. But that perpetual state of anxiety I'd been trying to outrace had just caught back up with me. No, I scolded myself. I won't let myself go there. Things are fine. Everything is fine.

I dropped my books in the locker and plucked my hefty economics tome from the bottom of the stack. Slamming the flimsy metal door I turned to find Leonard waiting patiently, his arms behind his back. The halls were still filled with students changing classes, and a few glanced at us, oddly, as Lenny revealed his gift: a giant bouquet of fake plastic roses that were somehow illuminated and glowed various colors, morphing from blue to purple to orange to yellow. It was a garish sight to behold.

"They're battery-powered," he said, his tone triumphant. "I wanted to get you something that would actually last, because that's how I feel about our relationship." Our relationship?

"Lenny, wow. I don't know what to say." I really didn't know what to say.

"And would you believe a dozen of these suckers was actually cheaper than if I'd bought you a dozen of the real thing? I knew you'd appreciate my delivering them in person, too. I got one like this for your prom corsage." Oh no, he didn't. As more bystanders stood in the hallway gawking at us, my humiliation grew.

"Yeah, well, Lenny, that's still a few months off," I said. "You might change your mind—"

"That's like saying the Cubs might win the pennant this year," he said. "Not gonna happen."

"Okay." I managed a weak smile. "I've got to get to class." I could feel the roses lighting up my face from blue to purple to orange to yellow. Could this banner day get any worse?

If there was ever an occasion that merited skipping class, today was it. No way could I make it through economics class, and what was I supposed to do with these roses? Mr. Richter had a pottery class this period, and I didn't have time before the bell to slip unnoticed into the darkroom. Damn. It would have to be the girls' bathroom near the cafeteria, which should be empty this time of day.

I was relieved to find that no one else seemed to have had the same idea. You could have heard a pin drop in the windowless bathroom, which was at the end of a long hallway, off the radar of school staff at this time of day. I guiltily shoved the technicolor roses into the trash can, then went into the last of the six stalls, dropped the lid on the toilet, and sat down to write in my journal. I had a flood of thoughts going through my brain and knew the best way to excise them was to write everything out and then try to forget about it. I'd only just written the date on the page when I heard the outer bathroom door swing open. I froze and lifted up my feet. The last thing I needed was to get caught playing hooky.

"But I don't understand," said a voice that sounded eerily similar to Beth's. "Why do you hate me so much?"

"You know *exactly* why." That was Kristy. Her tone of voice meant business.

"No I don't!" Beth said.

"Try telling that to my absentee boyfriend."

"Duff? Is *that* what this is about?"

"That, yes, among other things. And just because you've been acting batshit crazy since Duncan's death doesn't mean I'm just going to forgive and forget."

"Kristy, wait!" I heard the door swing open and shut again. Kristy must have left, but I could still hear Beth. She was sobbing now, loudly. I peaked under the stall door and saw her collapse to her knees on the grungy tile floor. What was wrong with her? I decided to make a break for it before things got weirder. I quietly opened the stall door. When she turned and saw me, Beth's wailing got louder, almost to the point of hyperventilating. But it was the look on her face that stopped me in my tracks. I don't know that I've ever witnessed such agony in another human being's eyes before. It sent shivers down my spine, but also compelled me to show her an ounce of compassion.

"Beth!" I stooped down to the ground and gripped her upper arms in my hands, hoping to shake some sense into her. "Beth, what's gotten into you?"

"I ruined everything," she said in a near rasp, looking up at me with an expression that seemed almost innocent, like a little girl who'd just gotten caught playing with matches. "My hands are not clean," she said, her voice barely audible. She was shivering now, so I reached for her cheerleader jacket, which was slung over her purse on the floor. She cradled the coat to her chest like it was a baby, rocking it back and forth as her limp blonde hair hung over her face. Then it happened. Our eyes both landed on that same red pinprick, the spot I'd seen in the moonlight after the party. The spot of . . . was it really blood?

"Oh my god!" she said, looking at me and then back to the coat with a ghastly, horrified expression. She jumped to her knees, turned on the faucet, and shoved the coat under the soap dispenser, letting a huge puddle of pink liquid drizzle over it. She started rubbing furiously at the wool and leather coat with her bare hands until they were raw and chafed. "It won't come clean!" She seemed to forget I was there as she scrutinized her coat. "He's dead and buried, so why is he still here? Why is the spot still here?" She was freaking out so completely by this point that I felt sure an adult would be swooping in any second to investigate the commotion. I decided to bolt before that happened. Any armchair psychologist could figure out why Beth was going bonkers, and while I was definitely concerned about her state of mind, it was also hard for me to feel completely sorry for her.

CHAPTER FIFTEEN

This Place Is Too Cold for Hell

STAMPING MY FEET ON THE SNOW didn't seem to help much, but I did it anyway in the hopes of warming up my toes. With the wind-chill factor, it must have been somewhere around minus-four degrees outside. Brief patches of sun offered a little relief when the clouds were feeling generous, but my thick ski gloves made picture-taking problematic. It was easier for me to pull off one glove with my teeth and try to adjust the aperture until my bare hand became too raw and chapped to stand it. Luckily, there were enough people squeezed in around me that they blocked a little of the wind as we waited on the curb.

"Kingston! Hey!" I looked up and saw Cat, Kaya, and Tess tromping down the street, laughing their asses off. If the cold was bothering them, they didn't show it.

"Aren't you guys freezing?" I asked. "I'm a human Popsicle!"

"It's a cauldron in here," said Tess, tapping her down-filled parka. "It's all about dressing in layers. Traps the heat."

"You scored a primo spot!" Cat said. "Scooch." I pushed a little to my left to make room for the three of them. The older woman standing next to me sighed loudly, obviously annoyed with me.

"I was saving this spot for my friends," I said, only semi-apologetically.

The sidewalks were jam-packed for several blocks with spectators awaiting the annual Running of the Reindeer, an event modeled after the Running of the Bulls in Pamplona, Spain. A herd of deer gets unleashed on a street full of people who, in turn, run for their lives. Only the truly undaunted participate in the run, although there's never really any fear of being mauled—reindeer antlers are velvety soft, and besides, they curve inward. Those of us not interested in taking our chances lined the streets to watch.

I'd been hanging out with Cat and the girls more often in recent weeks, which had gone a long way in helping me feel like the new year was off to an okay start. I was grateful to them for including me in their small group, even though I knew I'd never really be as tight with them as they already were with each other. In any case, I was enjoying my late-in-the game transition from loner to "one of the girls." It was different for me, but fun.

"This is my second latte this afternoon," Kaya said with a giggle, her bare hands wrapped around a plastic-lidded cardboard cup. "I am soooo wired!"

"When does this dog-and-pony show get on the road, anyway?" Cat said, craning her neck to see down Fourth Avenue.

"Should be any minute now." I noticed she had a slight grimace on her face. "Everything cool?"

"Oh, just reveling in the irony of it all," she said. "A bunch of reckless hooligans, drunk, no doubt, thinking it'd be fun to outrace a pack of wild animals."

"Such the 'white-man' way," Tess said while idly scrolling through her cell phone.

"Okay. . . ." Since I didn't quite get their drift, I started checking out my camera again, making sure there was no condensation on the lens.

"Don't get me wrong," Cat said. "I'm totally stoked to gawk alongside everyone else. But this pretty much flies in the face of everything our people believe about nature."

"Oh, here she goes—'Eskimo lecture time,'" Kaya said with a sigh. Cat ignored her.

"You don't try to conquer nature, let alone try to outrun it . . . you just plain don't mess with it, that's all."

"Hey, Cat, we heard it *ad nauseum* on the way here in the car. We *get* it." Kaya jokingly rolled her eyes and took another sip of her latte. "You're preaching to the choir."

"All I'm saying is, the minute you think you can outsmart life, that's when life will outsmart you. Next thing you know, you've got a reindeer nose up your ass."

"What would prompt somebody to want to outrun a reindeer, anyway?" I said.

"To tempt fate," said Cat. "No one can ever just accept their life for what it is."

"Meaning what?"

"Meaning everyone is looking for the next big thrill to feel alive, chasing the unattainable. They think they're standing apart from the crowd, when really they're just one of the pack." I decided not to remind her that the event was a charity fundraiser since I didn't sense that she was likely to concede her point.

"I hear a drum!" said Kaya. "Does that mean it's starting?"

The start of the race was located a half-mile down the road and around a corner, so we couldn't see much. Suddenly, the crowd's low muffle turned into shouts, laughter, and gasps. I looked through my camera's viewfinder expecting to see a mad-dash of jogging frat boys enter the frame. Instead, who should round the corner but our own Jenna Powell! Cat put her fingers to the corners of her mouth and let out a piercing whistle.

"Get a load of her!" Kaya placed both of her hands on my shoulders and jumped, apparently hoping it would give her a boost to see more.

"I can't see anything!" she said. "What's happening?"

Jenna was waltzing down the street waving like a pageant girl who'd just received the crown, only instead of a tiara, fake felt reindeer antlers were perched on her head. Over her red bikini she wore a sash that said, "Stop the cruelty" and she hoisted a sign on a wooden pole that read, "Beers and Deers Don't Mix." She managed to sashay her way halfway up the street to the sound of catcalls, jeers, and a smattering of applause, until, finally, a chubby police officer jogging behind her caught up and escorted her off the street.

Kaya and Tess were busting a gut by now, while I snapped as many pictures as I could. Jillian would high-five me for this on Monday.

"Deers, *plural*?!" Tess was almost crying with laughter. "Oh my god, and she plans on graduating in four more months? That is so sad!"

"Something is not right in that girl's head," remarked the lady next to me.

"You've got to give the chick credit," said Kaya. "*She* doesn't follow the herd mentality!"

Before I could respond, another surge of cheering erupted from down the block. The reindeer had officially been let loose. Rounding the corner, a throng of hundreds of runners looked like they were just unleashed from a house of horrors. They'd each paid thirty bucks (no pun intended) for the privilege of participating. Many wore stupid costumes. As they passed by our block, I snapped a picture of one guy with a bunch of carrots tied to his ass and the words "come and get me" written on the back of his shirt. I took pictures of people slipping in the snow and landing flat on their face. I took pictures of the reindeer weaving stealthily through the crowd. Despite Jenna's fears, they didn't seem much the worse for wear compared with their human counterparts. The runners and reindeer all came and went in under a minute. That was that. People immediately started to mill about on the street or head for their cars.

"How anticlimactic," said Kaya. "I could barely see anything anyway."

"You didn't miss much. What should we do now?" Tess threaded her arm through mine.

"There's a plate of chicken fingers with my name on it at the Hurlyburly," Cat said. "Who's in?"

I smiled, glad to be a part of their camaraderie. Tess rode in my car on the way there, and we talked about our plans for after graduation.

"I'm thinking about double-majoring in chemistry and math, but it depends on where I'm accepted," she rambled as I concentrated on the icy road. "But then I also would love to minor in fine arts, so who knows?"

"Speaking of fine arts, what are you gonna do for Richter's end-of-semester senior project?"

"Oh, don't remind me!" she said, sighing. "As if we don't have enough to do studying for the AP tests and everything else?"

Mr. Richter had dropped the bombshell a few weeks ago, assigning a final project for an end-of-the-year exhibition. It would account for seventy percent of our final grade. In June, we'd have to turn in original pieces that we felt best signified our experience at East Anchorage High over the past four years.

"I think maybe I'll glue an Extra Strength Tylenol onto a canvas and call it a day," Tess teased. "That would about sum up my high school career."

I double-parked behind Kaya's car outside the Hurlyburly; the lot was full.

"Looks like everybody had the same idea," Tess said, as she bounded up the front wooden deck and pushed through the door. I followed her in. A bunch of older men lined the bar stools; permanent fixtures here, I presumed. Cat waved us over to the red vinyl booth she and Kaya managed to nab. We piled all our coats, scarves, and mittens in the far corner and gazed at the sauce-smudged menus.

"Uh, yeah, can I have a side-order of crud with that?" Kaya cringed, wiping her side of the table down with a napkin. Just then Easy himself showed up and plunked four red plastic cups of ice water down on the table.

"Evenin', gals. What can I do ya for?" We decided to split two orders of chili cheese fries, a plate of chicken fingers, and a small cheese pizza.

"And just water for me," I said, worried that he might add a little something fifteen-proof to any other beverage. I spied Craig and a bunch of his friends on the other side of the room, but did my best not to let my eyes wander back in that direction. As much as I tried to ignore him, every fiber of my being was aware of his proximity. Apparently, Kaya had gotten the same view.

"Cool kid alert—oh my gosh, I can't believe I forgot!" she exclaimed, leaning closer to the middle of the table. "Goss-*ip*!" The rest of us moved in to hear. "So, did you guys notice how Beth Morgan missed a bunch of school last week? I overheard Mrs. Sheridan and Mrs. Kimball talking about it yesterday afternoon. Apparently, she's got some kind of eating disorder."

"Like anorexia or something?" Tess leaned in to hear amidst the din.

"Her dad checked her into a rehab facility, where she's been all week. They said she was supposed to be getting out today, so I guess she'll be back at school on Monday."

"Jeez," said Cat, sweeping her hands through the new blue streak in her hair and crunching on some ice from her water glass.

"That's strange," Tess said. "I thought eating disorders mostly affected people who feel powerless. They starve themselves, or whatever, as a way of restoring some semblance of control."

"Beth doesn't come across that way," said Cat. "She's a bitch, for sure, but that girl rules with an iron fist."

"Maybe her rationale is pure vanity," said Kaya.

I didn't say anything, but I knew that Beth had good reason to feel as though her life were spiraling out of control. Thank god that wasn't me.

• • •

Too many greasy French fries had given me a minor stomach ache by the time I pulled into our driveway, well under my curfew time, I noted. But when I came through the front door, Mom and Dad were both sitting at the kitchen table staring at me. They didn't look angry, but they didn't look happy, either. I checked the clock on our DVR box in the living room.

"What?" I said in a huff. "It's only ten-thirty! I wasn't doing anything wrong!"

"We know that, Skye," Mom said. "But we'd like you to sit down with us. We need to have a talk."

"Did something happen to Ollie?" I panicked.

"No, no," Dad said. "He's in bed asleep." Okayyyy. . . . Soooooo? I wracked my brains for any apparent reasons they might have been pissed with me. Excluding my little secret from the night at the hunting shack—which they couldn't have known anything about—I couldn't figure out what I'd done. They waited for me to walk to the sink and fill a glass of water at the tap. I stared at them while drinking it down. The mood was getting more somber by the minute. Mom looked as if she was about to bust out bawling and Dad wouldn't make eye contact with me. I finally placed my glass in the dishwasher and joined them at the table.

"Babydoll," Mom said. "Your dad and I have been trying to figure out how best to break the news to you, and I'm afraid there's just no way of saying this that's going to be easy for you to hear." I felt every fiber of my body freeze. My heart started thumping loudly in my chest and I began to breathe more rapidly. "For some time now," Mom continued, "Your dad and I have felt like our relationship has changed from what it was when we first met and fell in love. Your father and I have decided—" Oh God.

"Stop! Don't!" I said, bursting into sobs.

"Oh, baby. . . . " Mom was crying now, too. "Your dad and I. . . ."

"QUIT SAYING 'YOUR DAD!'" I shouted. "He's YOUR HUSBAND!" Nobody said anything for a few seconds, but then my dad lifted his head. He looked agonized.

"Skye-bear, we're still a family no matter what. We'll always be a family, and nothing changes that. Your mom . . . *Mom* and I will always love each other, but our family is going to be a lot more happy and a lot more healthy if we don't remain married to one another."

"But I thought you *were* happy." I could feel my lower lip turn down. The ugly-crying face was setting in and snot was hanging out of my nose. "What about Christmas? Everything was great!"

"Skye, we're so sorry," Mom said. "We're so sorry to be hurting you. But we're thinking about what's best for you and Ollie." The thought of Ollie growing up handed back-and-forth between two different homes like a Ping-Pong ball filled me with rage.

"Oh, what's best for us?" I said, snapping at her. "Were you thinking about what was best for us when you were off cheating on Dad with some stranger every Tuesday night when we thought you were working?" Mom stared down at the table, but Dad stood up and looked angry now.

"You watch your mouth, missy."

"I don't HAVE TO, because this conversation is OVER!" I kicked back my chair, which fell over onto the kitchen floor. After storming to my bedroom I slammed the door shut with a force that shook the house. It must have woken Ollie, because he started crying from the bedroom next door. He cried himself back to sleep. So did I.

CHAPTER SIXTEEN

Screw Your Courage to the Sticking Place

I WOKE UP ON MY BED, FULLY DRESSED, still in my boots. The alarm clock on my nightstand glowed twelve-thirteen. My pillow was totally damp from where I'd been crying. There was no way I was going to be able to go back to sleep. Remembering the awful conversation with my parents, I wondered why all this was happening. I'd been staring at a refrigerator magnet of a cartoon tooth when my mom had broken the news. The tooth had a smiley face and the number of our family dentist on it. It was stuck on the fridge holding up a "Buy one, get one free" coupon for Kraft Singles. Weird the things you notice when your world is crashing down around you.

I sighed deeply. My chest ached like someone had been sitting on it. My face felt hot and my eyelids were puffy. What was going to happen now? Would Mom move into her skeevy-jerk boyfriend's house? Would Dad have to rent a crummy apartment on the other side of town? Could they even *afford* to get divorced? Was this the death knell for my chances of going away to college? I knew it was selfish to think that way, but goddammit, *they* were the selfish ones! You don't just tear a family apart on a whim; you find a way to make it work. Why did they even *have* Ollie in the first place if they were "falling out of love" or whatever bullshit they're claiming?

117

The thoughts running through my head felt like a physical, tangible pain. I was desperate to make it go away. But where could I escape to in the dead of night? Nowhere. I wasn't close enough with Cat or Kaya or Tess to dump this on them. Besides, they were probably all asleep. I turned on my nightstand and retrieved my journal from my messenger bag, along with a Bic pen, thinking writing might help. But my eyes were too blurred with tears to even see the lines on the notebook paper. Besides, I felt more like stabbing the pen through my thigh than actually using it for its intended purpose.

I chucked the pen and the journal across the room and eyed my cell sitting on the nightstand. I couldn't. I mean, I definitely, DEFINITELY *shouldn't*. This was one of those you'll-hate-yourself-in-the-morning moments, on par with drunk-dialing an ex-boyfriend. But even though we technically weren't on speaking terms, Craig was the closest thing to a true confidante I'd ever had. He'd been at the Hurlyburly when I left, so he might still be awake. It was only a little past midnight, after all. My brain was screaming "bad idea!" as I grabbed my cell and started to punch in the numbers, but then I remembered *his* cell hidden deep in my closet. He might have a different number now. The chance that I'd get a "We're sorry," recording from the phone company gave me nerve enough to hit the call button. Ninety percent of me was praying he didn't answer so I could just hang up and keep my self-respect. But that other ten percent, that part of me that was so desperate for a lifeline, prayed for the sound of his voice.

By the fourth ring, my brain had gotten back in the game and I realized what a colossal mistake I was making. I was about to hang up when he picked up.

"Skye?" I panicked. Now what? I hadn't planned on what I would actually say to him had he answered, genius that I was. "Uh, *hellooo*?" he said. "Skye? Is that you?"

"You're awake!"

"Obviously. . . . ?" He was waiting for me to explain myself.

"I'm sorry to bother you this late, but I saw you at the bar earlier, and—"

"You were there?" Ouch. While I was pretending not to see him, he hadn't noticed me at all.

"Um, yeah. So anyway, I'm sorry to bug you. I just was feeling like I really needed somebody I could talk to."

"Are you drunk?" There was no misinterpreting the surprise and skepticism in his voice.

"No! Of course not!" Oh god. Now I was really embarrassed. I shouldn't have called. "Are you?"

"Am I what?"

"Drunk?"

"I wish."

"Okay," I said. "Well, you're probably thinking it's strange that I'm calling you, but I'm just . . . freaking out right now, and—"

"What in the hell does *she* want?" It was Beth's voice, now, in the background.

"Oh." My heart was officially, in that instant, broken to smithereens. "I guess I thought you were alone."

"Hold on," he said. I considered just hanging up in the interim, as I heard low, indistinguishable murmurs. He must have had his hand cupped over the receiver. Finally Beth raised her voice. "Tell your stalker that she has a really annoying habit of turning up at all the wrong times." Great. What had I interrupted this time?

"Skye?" Craig was back on the line now.

"You know what, I'm going to go." I was crying now, humiliated, hurt, and angry with myself for being so pathetic.

"Wait!" Craig said. "Is everything okay? What's wrong?"

"Nothing you can fix," I said, before shutting my phone.

It vibrated several times that night as I lay awake in my bed. He'd left one voicemail and several texts: "Pick up," "RUOK?" and "????" By three-fifteen he had stopped trying. I finally drifted back to sleep two hours later.

On Monday at school, I avoided him like the plague. Beth was right about my stalker tendencies. I pretty much knew where all of Craig's classes were, which helped me to circumnavigate any hallways where I might potentially cross his path. Unfortunately, I still had to see Beth in class, but I managed not to make eye contact with her, and she didn't say a word to me. No doubt, she was just trying to stay under the radar given her recent stint at Hotel Anorexia. She looked paler than usual, and definitely gaunt. I ate my lunch in the newspaper office to avoid seeing either her or Craig in the caf. Jillian came in the office while I was picking at my turkey sandwich.

"What are you doing in here?" she asked. I shrugged, but tossed her the prints of Jenna from the Reindeer Run.

"Oh my god, *score!*" she said with a laugh. "Wow, that girl is certifiable."

I'd gotten up at five o'clock in the morning so I wouldn't have to run into my parents at home. The maintenance man and I were the first people on the school premises, and I'd headed straight to the darkroom to develop the pictures. The day before, I'd muttered a few brief grunts to my Mom and Dad before heading to the Regent for a John Hughes movie marathon, half of which I'd slept through. I'd returned home after dinner and gone straight to my bedroom. I knew that I'd have to interact with my parents eventually, but I wasn't ready for that just yet.

"How was the Running of the Reindeer?" asked Jillian. I shrugged my shoulders again. "Okay, Grumps. I can take a hint." Just then Leonard and Megan walked in, bickering as usual.

"All I'm saying is, I don't think golf is really an athletic pursuit," Megan said in a griping tone. "I mean, you might as well say that billiards is a sport."

"Some people *do* say that," Leonard said, rolling his eyes until they landed on me. "Well, if it isn't Skye Kingston, my one and only future prom date, looking exceptionally gorgeous on this Monday—!"

"Zip it, Lenny," Jillian said. "She's not in the mood." I continued to sulk over my sandwich.

"That's how I like my ladies." Lenny was unrelenting, placing his hand on my shoulder. "Feisty, not flirty."

"Lenny," Jillian said, "there's pepper spray on my keychain that is meant for molesters. Don't tempt me into using it." Lenny made a dramatic point of lifting his hand off my shoulder before bowing in deference to our editor.

"Sorry, Skye." He leaned in and whispered amicably in my ear. "I didn't mean anything by it."

"I was going to tell you at the meeting this afternoon, but I guess I can spill it now," Jillian said. "A reliable source down at police headquarters told one of the guys at the *Daily News* that there might be a break in the case."

"Do you think they have a suspect?" Megan asked. I listened intently.

"I don't know anything beyond that," Jillian answered.

Suddenly my appetite was shot. I stuffed the rest of my sandwich in my brown paper lunch bag and crushed it into a ball. As if I really needed another reason not to cross paths with Craig today. I tried to repeat the mantra "not my problem" as I left for my next class, but it was hardly convincing.

CHAPTER SEVENTEEN

Your Face Is as a Book Where Men May Read Strange Matters

THE DAYS WERE BEGINNING TO STAY LIGHTER, longer. The snow had melted from sidewalks and parking lots, though there were still thawing patches on the grass. An epidemic of senioritis was underway at school as we officially started to count down not just the months but the weeks and days we had left. That was good news for most, but bad news for me, as I spent most of my waking hours studying for my AP exams with the ultimate aim of getting advanced college credit. They were supposedly going to be brutal if the horror stories from last year's seniors were to be believed. Considering my collegiate future was pretty much in limbo, I had to wonder why I was even bothering. Worse still, I had yet to figure out what to turn in for my final project in Richter's art class. I had enough photographs from the past four years to fill a tractor-trailer, but were any really momentous enough to encapsulate my high school experience?

As I poured over my boxes of prints in the darkroom, it occurred to me that my high school career had merely been spent as an observer, looking from the outside in. Of course, it goes without saying that I wasn't in any of my own photos—pictures of pep rallies and football games, student council meetings and amateurish musical productions—but that was my problem entirely. To judge from these photos, I never even went to this school. I didn't exist. I silently cursed our English teacher for assigning Camus's *The Stranger* as end-of-year reading. The last thing I needed, with all my other problems, was existential angst. But seriously, beyond hiding behind my camera for the *Polar Bear Post*, what had I really involved myself in at this school? What was my clique? Where were the candid shots of me, laughingly roaming the halls or crowding into a group photo at a school dance?

Speaking of dances, ugh. Lenny. Prom was fast approaching, and every time I thought about his hands around my waist during some cheesy rock ballad, I wanted to barf. When he'd asked me in October to be his date, it didn't seem real, but now that it was staring me in the face, it was hard to pretend away. He was a nice enough guy, if only he didn't try so hard or lust after me in such a completely goober-faced way. Letting him down semi-gently wasn't working, so at some point I would have to make Lenny understand that, prom or no prom, romance wasn't in the cards for us; not now, not ever.

By this time I had restored minimal interaction with my parents, but I'd hardly call myself Suzy Sunshine with regards to their split. In March, Mom had moved into a condo with some chick she went to school with. She occasionally still dropped in for dinners and we had prearranged visits with her on the weekends, which usually involved wandering around the mall for a few hours, followed by lunch. Dad stayed at the house with us, and while he was at work, Ollie got dropped off at a neighbor's daycare. Even though I blamed Mom for most of this, I still hadn't wanted to reward my dad by granting him any normal-seeming father-daughter chats. Instead, I continued to make a habit of going to school at the crack of dawn rather than engage him with forced pleasantries over the breakfast table. I sat in the school library from six-thirty to seven-fifty every morning, sharing the space with mostly freshmen who'd been dropped off by parents on their way to work. Currently, three freshmen girls with enough metalwork in their mouths to cage a lion were giggling behind me. They were hunched over a table perusing *Lady Chatterley's Lover* for the sex scenes, and their titilated outbursts were making it hard for me to concentrate on my calculus questions.

It was seven-forty. Odds were, my homeroom door would be unlocked by now, so I tossed my textbook in my bag and headed for the hallway. No sense listening to those prepubescent Mouseketeers if I didn't have to. As I passed by the cafeteria, Kristy Winters emerged and her face lit up at the sight of me. *Random.* What was all this about?

"Oh good! Come with me." She grabbed my arm and led me down a row of lockers. "I'm trying to round up all the seniors today," she explained. We stopped at her locker, where she brought out a stiff manila envelope. "These are the proofs for the yearbook. Oh, hey, Craig! Wait up!" I turned around and saw Craig walking by, his eyes still groggy with sleep. He had a granola bar in his hand and a small carton of milk. We glanced at each other before he looked, vacantly, at Kristy.

"I was looking for you," she said. "The yearbook staff needs everyone to sign something. Oh wait, let me find my Sharpie."

While Kristy dug around in her backpack for her wayward marker, Craig and I waited in silence. "Did you guys hear about Duff?" she smiled at us, still digging around through her bag's various zippered compartments. "He's on his way back from Scotland! Good thing, too, because I told him he'd be in the doghouse, bigtime, if I had to fly solo at prom. I found out just in time, because the King and Queen nominations are due tomorrow. Sorry, Craig," she said with a wink, "but you've got some competition now." Craig looked decidedly uninterested.

"Oh duh!" Kristy exclaimed, finally noticing the Sharpie pen clipped onto one of her folders. She slid the contents out from the oversized manila envelope. "We just thought this would be a nice gesture for the yearbook, if everyone could write a special thought or memory." She shoved two sheets of oversized paper in front of Craig. In the center of one sheet were the words, "Forever Missed, Forever Loved." On the other piece of paper was Duncan's class picture from junior year. There were already several marker-inscribed epitaphs on the pages, including one, I noticed, signed by Beth: *"Good night, sweet prince."*

"It's going to be a two-page spread," continued Kristy, "so write anywhere you can find a . . . *Dammit, Craig! Watch what you're doing!"*

Craig's carton of milk had dropped—*THWAP!*—on the linoleum floor and exploded, spraying my legs, his shoes, and the bottom of four lockers. Kristy snatched Duncan's memorial pages back. "Thanks a lot, Craig! You almost destroyed it."

"I already did." Craig said under his breath, to no one in particular. "I destroyed everything." I found a packet of Kleenex in my bag and started soaking up some of the offending two-percent. He stooped down next to me.

"Are you okay?" I asked. He didn't answer as we continued mopping up the mess.

. . .

A migraine would have been preferable to the current plague wreaking havoc on my brain, and Kristy's lunchtime performance wasn't helping. Gloating to her group of friends, she had stood up from the table, grabbed a spoon for a microphone, and started singing "My Boyfriend's Back," that smug and saccharine pop song from the sixties. Great God almighty. I had immediately scanned the caf to find Beth, who no longer held a place of honor at Kristy's table. She had begun sitting with Craig and the hockey team several months ago. Not that she even needed a lunch break. I'd been paying attention ever since her return from the anorexia resort. She'd made a show of ordering a meal since the teaching staff was keeping an eye on her, but she only ever seemed to push the food around on her plate.

Kristy's antics across the room caught the attention of both Beth and Craig. Beth had a serious scowl on her face, which wasn't all that unusual these days, but Craig looked like death warmed over.

"Look at those two," Tess said, taking a break from tying knots in her straw wrapper. "They look deranged."

"*That's* our future Prom King and Queen?" Cat said. "Do they even make straight jackets with sequins?"

Cat had a good point. Beth and Craig were both trying to pretend like it was business as usual, but everyone in school had figured out by this point that they were seriously jacked-up. Beth ambled around school like she was sleepwalking and Craig now sported a hair-trigger temper. He'd gotten detention three times in the last month for mouthing off to teachers. "Do you know who I am?" he had demanded of Principal Schaeffer just last Wednesday. "My father could *buy* this school."

Driving home that afternoon that stupid song Kristy had been singing at lunch was still stuck in my head. I flipped stations on the car radio in the hopes of finding another tune to dislodge this one from my brain. All commercials. Figures. Kristy wasn't the only person at school who seemed excited that Duff was homeward bound. In his first three years at East Anchorage, he had enjoyed an unparalleled popularity. Yes, he was good-looking and one of the cool crowd, but it was more than just that. He was the king of afterschool activities, playing on the hockey team, starring in school plays, helping tutor remedial freshmen, planning "*fiestas locas*" with the Spanish club. He even used to turn up at Jenna's sparsely attended environmental pep rallies. He'd positioned himself as a good-natured, charismatic everyman, and I'd never heard anyone badmouth him. Now, people were getting stoked about his return. From what I'd been hearing today, he had completed his schooling in Scotland and was coming home so that he could participate in the end-of-year seniorpalooza with the rest of us. Kristy had accused Beth of being behind Duff's exile, but whatever had prompted him to be shipped off in the first place didn't seem to be much of an issue now. Or was it? Kristy's boyfriend was coming back, just like the song said. And as the lyrics cautioned, I wondered if trouble could be far behind.

I pulled into my driveway, wishing I could swing by Ollie's daycare and pick him up early. Too bad I didn't have his car seat. The weather was still so beautiful that I considered walking over with his stroller to get him. Before making my way to the front door, I stopped to check the mailbox. It was jammed full. Catalog, catalog, bill, junk, junk, bill. . . . University of Southern California? My heart stopped. It was a thin envelope. My heart sank. Oh well, there are still my Plan Bs, I reassured myself. I stuck the rest of the mail under my armpit and ripped open the letter. My heart soared:

Dear Ms. Kingston:

We are pleased to inform you that you have been accepted into the undergraduate program at the University of Southern California. Based on the strength of your SAT scores, combined with your high school transcripts and application essay, we believe you would be an asset to the USC Trojan family. We are prepared to offer you the Julia Ann Fowler Women in Fine Arts Scholarship, in the hopes that you will very seriously consider USC as you weigh your college options.

A packet of materials will be mailed out to you in the next several weeks with more detailed information.

Our very best wishes to you for a successful collegiate experience, and I sincerely hope you will be joining us in the fall.

Sincerely,

Joanna Nussbaum
Admissions Officer

P.S. We were particularly impressed by the photography submissions included in your application.

Certainly, there would still be some numbers to crunch, but all at once my college dream was suddenly within reach. Remember in *The Wizard of Oz*, when Dorothy was having a tough time of it, but she finally caught her first glimpse of The Emerald City and everything was sunshine-y and cool? That was me right now. Then again, meeting the Wizard didn't exactly solve all of Dorothy's problems, did it?

CHAPTER EIGHTEEN

Why Do You Dress Me in Borrowed Robes?

I RANG THE DOORBELL AT MOM'S CONDO TWICE before her roommate, Margot, finally answered. Her hair was wrapped in a fluffy green towel, and she was wearing jeans and a ratty old CBGB T-shirt. She was twenty-five years old, and Mom had found her on the college's housing message board. I'd met her twice before, briefly, but this was the first time I'd actually visited their apartment. I was there because Mom had promised to take me shopping for a prom dress. I'd put it off as long as possible, and Leonard had finally given up on harassing me about it, but now that it was the weekend before prom I knew I had to get it over with or risk having to wear a duct tape dress to the big night.

"Come on in," Margot said, leading me down the long hallway decorated with framed punk records from the seventies and into the living room, which was cozy in a haphazard, lived-in way: mismatched furniture and a shelving unit shoddily constructed out of two-by-fours and cinder blocks. A rats' nest of power cords and cables dangled from behind the makeshift entertainment center, which consisted of an ancient-looking TV and CD player. I recognized the patchwork quilt hanging over the back of the couch; it was the one that had always been draped across the bottom of the bed in my parents' room.

"Your mom should be back from the Laundromat any minute," Margot explained, motioning me toward the couch. It was so weird that she was closer to my age than my mom's. I was again reminded of the fact that my mom was living a completely different life than the one she'd had when we were still a family, as if she was trying to reclaim her youth and pretend to be some cool college kid. A scary thought, and one that made me yearn for the "good old days," as imperfect as they'd been. Sometimes when I thought about the future, I couldn't picture anything at all. It was like stepping off a space station and floating away into nothingness.

Margot pulled the towel off, tipped her head, and starting drying the roots, which were purposefully darker than the rest of her hair. She had an edgy cut that really suited her. Great to see Mom had traded me in for this more compelling counterpart. I accepted Margot's offer of soda, and while she went to get it, I took the opportunity to check out the large oil painting hanging over the brick fireplace.

It was a riff on the classic *American Gothic* painting of the grumpy, hayfork wielding farmer and his equally stern wife. Only in this image the weathered man in the portrait was holding a whaling spear. When I was twelve, I'd seen the original masterpiece up close at the Art Institute of Chicago while visiting my grandparents. Mom's father was a professor of art history and his docent friend had given us a private tour of the museum. Gramps never passed up an opportunity to educate us and had also used the painting as a way to bring up his favorite topic, small-town mentality, which always seemed to upset Mom. He was a third-generation Chicagoan and didn't understood why his daughter had chosen to make her life in what he saw as a backwoods village with virtually no culture or real opportunity. In his eyes, Dad was to blame because he'd gotten one of those lucrative-but-dangerous fishing jobs here in the summers to pay his way through college. He'd quickly fallen in love with the vast open spaces and quirky types who call Alaska home. When he and Mom got married the summer after college, they moved to Anchorage, promising to reevaluate after three years. Of course, they never left.

"Like it?" asked Margot, interrupting my reverie.

"Yeah, it's intense," I said, taking the Diet Coke from her, "and really powerful." Oh god, could I sound any *more* lame?

"It was a class assignment." She settled down on the opposite end of the sofa, tucking her bare feet with black-painted toenails up under her knees, cross-legged.

"*You* painted this?" I had assumed that Margot was in pre-med with my mom. It had never occurred to me that she was an artist.

"Yep, I'm an art major," she explained. "Last semester we had to reinterpret a famous painting. I've always loved the original, so I decided to do an Alaska riff on it. It was either that or Munch's *The Scream*, but I thought that would be too 'junior high,'" she said.

"I like the way you think," I said with a laugh.

"Your mom says you're going to study photography?"

"Sort of. I got into the University of Southern California. . . ." Then I blurted out something I'd been thinking about since I received the acceptance letter. "But I don't know if I should go . . . with everything going on. My dad and Ollie need me."

"Did you talk to your parents about this?" From anyone else, this might have sounded pushy and condescending, but I could already tell that Margot had a knack for not sounding preachy.

"No." I shook my head reluctantly. "But they would just tell me to go."

"You're lucky they're so supportive," Margot said. "Everyone in my family is some sort of professional—doctors, lawyers, engineers, you name it. I decided to rock the boat and become a professional *artist*. I may as well have told them I was going to be a trapeze artist. Needless to say, they were not enthused."

"I know someone who is going through the same thing," I said, thinking of Craig and his dad.

"Hey, girls!" Mom came into the living room and plopped her heavy load of laundry down the on the couch. She looked exhausted but she had an enthusiastic smile on her face. "Skye, are you ready for some shopping? My treat, you know." She put her arms out for a hug and for the first time since she and Dad had broken the news to me, I actually gave her one.

• • •

Three hours later, I'd tried on just about every dress at three different department stores, to no avail. Everything either looked like something straight out of *Tacky Bridesmaid* magazine or it was way too short for my tall frame. I found two that might have actually worked, but once I'd glanced at the price tags, I pretended, for her bank account's sake, that they were the ugliest dresses on the planet.

"Are you sure, honey? It's actually quite becoming," Mom had said as I halfheartedly modeled a silver sequined cocktail dress with a plunging neckline in back.

"No, it's too glittery. I look like a deflated disco ball."

The light FM music being piped into the too-small dressing room was not helping the situation, and Mom was out of ideas. I texted Kaya for help and she suggested Savvy Seconds, assuring me that if there was still a decent-looking prom dress left in this city, the consignment shop would have it.

As we drove across town I crossed my fingers that the perfect dress would be waiting there for me. I tried to tell myself that it didn't matter, but who was I kidding? I couldn't help but get into the spirit of the whole thing. I'd seen all the movies: *Never Been Kissed, Pretty in Pink.* . . . Any kid with an ounce of cultural awareness knew the precedent for prom night. I was supposed to magically evolve from ugly duckling to glorious swan, making jaws everywhere hit the floor. But I didn't really care what anyone else thought. Only Craig. Even as I told myself I was completely over him, I wanted him to regret that he'd ever chosen Beth over me.

"Honey." My mom interrupted my Craig reverie. "There's something I wanted to talk to you about."

Uh oh. What now? Was she planning to marry a twenty-year-old? Or a fifty-year-old? Would I have stepbrothers?! Would she honestly expect me to be her maid of honor? I glanced outside the passenger window so she wouldn't have to see my face if I started to bawl.

"I overheard what you said to Margot about Dad and Ollie, and I need you to know something. A big part of the reason your dad and I split up was because of me."

"Duh, Mom, that's pretty clear." I said. She *was* having an affair and she was going to marry some jerk who'd want me to call him Dad. I just knew it.

"But maybe you don't understand why." You bet I understood. Late night study groups. Footsie underneath the table. Next thing you know, a family is completely destroyed.

"Your dad and I dated all the way through college. He was my first love," she said. "Right after we graduated, we moved here, and within a few months, I had you."

"Mom, I know all this. What's with the history lesson?" I rolled my eyes. I knew I was acting like a brat, but somehow I couldn't seem to stop punishing her, and she wasn't ready to stop me.

"I know you're thinking about staying in town to look after us," she said.

"I meant Dad and Ollie."

"I know you did."

Mom pulled into the mini mall parking lot and parked in front of Savvy Seconds. She shut off the engine and turned to me.

"Skye, you might not know this, but I had dreams, too." She put her hands in her lap and looked down at them thoughtfully. "From the time I was six years old I wanted to be a doctor. A surgeon, in fact. As I got older, I knew I was meant to save lives. In high school and college I took the most difficult science classes, and even though it didn't always come easy to me, I did really well."

"Yeah, so."

"So . . . your dad . . . you know how much he loves it here. From the first moment he saw it, he loved it down to his bones. I never did. I came here for him, and when he wanted to have a family, I chose to give up my dreams for a while. We decided I'd be a stay-at-home mom and be there for my girl when she came home from school." She reached out and took my hand.

"I love you, honey," she said, "but a part of me has always been missing. Now I'm doing what I'm meant to do."

"But didn't you want to have me?" My upper lip quivered. Here we go again, I thought. It seemed like I spent half the time on the brink of tears these days. Would things ever get better or was it always going to be like this?

"Of course, honey! I wanted you, and I wanted to be home with you." She sighed. "But there were other things I wanted, too. Your dad never understood. He thought I could just be happy with the way things were, the way *he* is. But I'm not that way. I need more. But this isn't about me. What I'm trying to say is, you need to follow your dreams. Do what your gut tells you, or you will resent your dad and Ollie. . . . It's not fair to you, and it's not fair to them." I opened the glove box and found a box of tissues. I handed one to Mom and took one for myself. The sound of us both sniffling into our Kleenex made me giggle and after a second Mom started laughing too.

"Mom, everything is going to be okay," I said reaching over to give her a hug. "It really is."

"I know, kiddo," she said, reaching for the door handle. "Now let's go find you a dress that will knock Craig's socks off."

"Am I that obvious?" I said as I hopped out of the car.

"I notice more than you think I do," she said giving me a strange look that made me wonder if she was referring to more than my gigantic crush. Nah, she couldn't be. . . .

CHAPTER NINETEEN

Stands Not Within the Prospect of Belief

MONDAY MORNING FOUND ME IN THE DARK-
ROOM completely immersed in my end-of-year photography
project, when Leonard tapped on the door. As usual he was sporting business casual attire: khaki pants, an argyle sweater vest, and
an oxford shirt. Oh no, I thought, what now? Would he want
to discuss pre-prom dinner options or—*quelle horreur!*—the after
party? I was totally ready to stop him then and there with a not-
so-gentle reminder that—as far as he knew—my curfew was still
midnight, no ifs, ands, or buts, when I realized he was looking a
little less confident than usual.

"Um, Skye," he said uneasily. "I was hoping to find you here.
We need to talk."

"What's up, Lenny?"

"I was just wondering if you'd purchased your prom dress yet."
Oh god, what was it with the cummerbund obsession?

"Yes, I got it this weekend, but—"

"Oh. That's too bad." He looked down at the floor, shuffling
his loafers against the cracked linoleum. "I know you were never
that excited about prom to begin with. . . ." he trailed off. "And
you said that if I changed my mind—"

"Lenny, what's going on?" I glanced at the nonexistent watch
on my wrist.

"Well, the thing is . . . " He paused again, infuriatingly. "Megan kinda sorta asked me to the prom over the weekend."

"Oh."

"So, I didn't think you'd mind so much if I went with her instead. But since you've already got the dress. . . . "

"No, sure, Lenny." Free at last, I thought, but not without a twinge of . . . something. Was I actually disappointed now that I was finally off the hook? I felt a lump forming in my throat, possibly more from embarrassment than anything. "That's okay, I can use the dress for lots of things: weddings, funerals, bat mitzvahs. It's really not a problem. You should go with Megan. You two will have a great time."

"Are you sure?"

"Positive." Lenny breathed an obvious sigh of relief. Jeez. Nothing like feeling as though you're a pair of heavy iron shackles on someone else's social life. Was I really such an inferior second to Megan?

"Thanks, Skye, I really appreciate it," he said holding out his hand. I put mine out and he gave it a shake as though we were business partners coming to an agreement. "No hard feelings?"

"None." I said, feigning enthusiasm. "Well, see you around."

"At the editorial meeting this afternoon, right?"

"Oh. Yeah. Sure."

Rejected by Leonard Livermore. That's what I'd gotten for being so cocky these last few weeks. Now I had a gorgeous dress, but no date. Oh well, I'd probably have a better time staying at home with Dad and Ollie on prom night. Lord knows the last time I'd attended a party I'd lived to regret it.

• • •

"Look, it's your senior year," said Tess, popping open a can of contraband soda, which recently had been outlawed, along with the once-ubiquitous candy machines, after the PTA got all riled up over an article about poor school nutrition in the *New York Times*. "You're sort of obligated to go. It's a 'rite of passage.'" Her silver bangles jangled as she formed quote marks with her hands.

Cat and Kaya nodded in agreement. Apparently the allure of prom had rubbed off on them in spite of their devil-may-care attitude about most school-related activities. As for my lack of a suitable escort, the girls couldn't have cared less. In fact, they insisted that going with a date was "patriarchal" and "sheep-like." As a matter of course, they were all going together. For the last couple of months I'd been sitting with them during lunch and had long since stopped feeling like the proverbial third, or in this case fourth, wheel. As much as I prided myself on my independence, it was nice to have a group of friends to rely on, and it didn't hurt that they actually seemed to appreciate my self-deprecating humor.

"It's not an option," agreed Cat. "You're hanging with us."

"We hereby decree." Kaya said.

"Okay," I said, taking a bite of my apple. "Since I don't have a choice. But I'm going under duress." I still felt a little awkward about the whole thing, but I realized *not* going meant Mom would have needlessly spent money on the dress. And besides, I think my mom was even more excited about the whole thing than I was.

"Now that that's settled, let's get back to where we left off yesterday," Kaya said, leaning in closer and lowering her voice to a loud whisper.

"Where were you yesterday?" I said.

"Oh, don't worry, Skye . . . we'll get to you soon enough." Kaya looked at me and giggled. "Cat, I believe it was your turn. . . ."

"Yes, what will it be, Cat?" said Tess, her eyes glinting mischievously. "Truth or dare?"

"As if I would actually submit myself to another one of your wicked dares," said Cat. "I still haven't emotionally recovered from the last mortification."

"Oh puh-leaze . . . an 'I Heart Fabio' poster taped on your locker—for one measly day—isn't even remotely the worst we could do."

"In that case, I'd much rather reveal a deep, dark secret this time around."

"Excellent," Kaya said.

"Okay, so you know Nick?" Cat said.

"Nick Horne?" I said, "Sure, he's on the hockey team."

"Yep," she said, pausing to make sure we were all attentive. "Well, I ran into him over the weekend at the video store."

"And?" Tess waved her hand in a get-to-the-point fashion.

"Well, turns out we were both looking for the same movie. You wouldn't know it, but Nick is quite the cinefile."

"That's your secret?" Kaya scoffed. "That doesn't count. If that's your secret, it's entirely unacceptable. You're going to have to do a dare instead."

"Wait," said Cat. "That's not it. My *secret* is that I kind of like him."

"Nick?" Kaya said, stunned, "Wait, what? A jock?"

"So what? He's more than a jock."

"Okay, tell us everything," Tess said. "When did you start liking him?"

As the girls whispered excitedly to one another, I grew lost in thought. It was my turn next. Would I choose a truth or a dare? Dares were out of the question. I couldn't stand to make myself vulnerable, possibly opening myself up to ridicule. But 'truth' was just as dicey. Although . . . maybe this was my last chance to finally let someone in on my truly deep, dark secret. If I told the girls what I'd overheard the night of Duncan's death, maybe they might have some good advice. At the very least I could get it off my chest, which would be a colossal relief. But what would they think of me for remaining quiet this whole time? Was it fair to burden them with what I knew?

"Skye," Kaya said, interrupting my train of thought. "We still have five minutes left before fifth period. Your turn." The girls looked at me expectantly.

"Actually, there is something I've been keeping from you," I said and inhaled deeply. "But this isn't a game, and it really—" Before I could finish the sentence, Kristy bounded up to our table and grabbed a chair next to Cat. I realized I was shaking slightly. I'd gotten so used to holding onto this secret that the thought of actually telling it was terrifying.

"Girls," Kristy said, "I just wanted to remind you that Duff and I are running for Prom King and Queen, and we'd really appreciate your vote." As if we could forget, I thought to myself. For weeks the halls and communal spaces had been plastered with candidate posters, and Kristy's were a blindingly hot pink.

"Actually I was planning to write in 'Marge and Homer Simpson,'" joked Cat, brandishing her soup spoon decisively in the air.

"Cute," Kristy said, not letting it sway her. Truth be told, I was almost beginning to like Kristy, when before I'd often wondered what a nice guy like Duff saw in her. She could take a joke at her own expense, and—in spite of her obsession with the trappings of popularity—she was clearly smarter than she let on. Ever since our chat the night of the party, she'd actually acknowledged me around school, which is more than I could say for most of the people in her social stratosphere. "Well, I'm just saying keep us in mind." She stood up to leave, but added, "Skye, the lip gloss looks great."

"Thanks," I said, still inwardly freaking about what I'd almost revealed to the girls. The clatter of a lunch tray crashing to the ground made us all start and crane our necks to the front of the cafeteria. An irate Beth stood screaming at Craig as they stood in the cafeteria line.

"*Goddammit, Craig.* Will you wake the hell up? This sweater is cashmere! You think ketchup just washes out, no problem? It's ruined!" Craig looked annoyed as he handed money to the cashier. "Get some napkins," Beth said.

"I'm not your freakin' personal assistant. Get them yourself!" Craig grabbed his tray from the counter, headed over to a table, and sat down with his back to Beth.

"I've never seen two people more destined to be King and Queen," Kaya said.

"They are seriously royal pains in the ass, and utterly perfect for each other," Tess said. Then, after getting a raised eyebrow from Cat, she added apologetically, "Sorry, Skye."

"That's okay," I said, hoping I sounded appropriately nonchalant "I couldn't care less. And you're right. They're totally a match made in hell." Just then the fifth bell rang out, and my friends started stacking their lunch trays and gathering up their belongings.

"Looks like you're saved by the bell, Skye," Cat said. "But don't think you're off the hook."

CHAPTER TWENTY

Be Bright and Jovial Among
Your Guests Tonight

"SKYE, JUST RELAX," Margot said as she aimed a mascara wand toward my left eye. "Look over my right shoulder and try not to blink." *Blink*? The left side of my face was spazzing out of control and I had to fight the urge to run screaming from the room like the totally mental wife in *Jane Eyre*.

The way my mom and Margot were acting, you'd think they'd been living for this moment their entire lives. All of their combined beauty products were arrayed on the bathroom counter, and Mom was waving a hot curling iron in the air as she danced around singing—no, make that shouting—along to Aretha Franklin's "Respect." Margot wiggled her butt to the chorus and I was terrified she'd poke my eye out.

When Mom had called to suggest that I get ready for prom with the two of them, I'd protested. I normally spent all of two minutes in front of the mirror, and that was when I remembered to brush my hair. But Mom was as persistent as the girls had been in convincing me to go in the first place, and Dad said he had to agree with her. Prom was making fools out of us all, I thought, giggling.

"So, honey," Mom said, putting the curling iron down and rifling through a selection of eye shadows. "What's the deal with this Craig guy? Has he wised up yet?"

"It's so over, Mom. . . ." I said with a sigh. "It's so over, it never even started." For once, I decided to stop pretending that I didn't care. It was exhausting keeping up a show of indifference and, with Mom at least, it wasn't working anyway.

"Well, you never know," Margot said. "Strange things can happen on prom night."

Mom nodded her head in agreement.

"I doubt it," I said. "His girlfriend wouldn't let him out of her sight. She's hellbent on their getting crowned Prom King and Queen, and I'm sure she'll be dragging him on the campaign trail up until the very last second."

"Who needs him, then?" Margot said. "I think it's great that you're going to the prom on your own. I guarantee you'll have more fun that way."

"Hear, hear," Mom said. "I am so proud of you! I only wish I'd been confident enough to do the same thing. Before I started dating your dad in high school, I ended up taking this guy named Marcus Finkey to the Christmas formal my sophomore year."

"Really?"

"He was my friend's younger cousin, and he had breath that could wilt flowers. He wore a purple tux, and he kept wanting to slow dance. I spent half the night in the bathroom trying to avoid him!"

"Oh god, that sounds like a nightmare," I said with laugh. "But hey, it's not like I'm the Joan of Arc of high school formals fending off paramours with a shield and sword. My options were limited."

"Some girls would spend the night moping in their room," said Mom, "But not my Skye-bear."

"What do you think," Margot said, turning to my mom. "Cream blush or powder?"

An hour later, I shimmied gingerly into the sapphire, almost-new gown that the manager of Savvy Seconds had brought from the back room for us the weekend earlier. Looking into the full-length mirror hanging on mom's bedroom door, I seriously felt like I was having an out-of-body experience. The dress hugged my frame in all the right places, almost as if it had been made for me. I turned and peered over my shoulder to check out the plunging back. Mom had pinned a white orchid to the side of my head, and my hair cascaded down in smooth waves. I could've sworn I'd been magically transformed into some sort of Pre-Raphaelite princess. It's amazing what a little makeup, a curling iron, and one hell of a dress could do, I decided.

I practically floated back to the bathroom where my fairy godmothers were waiting and had Margot zip me up. They fawned over how much bluer the dress made my eyes look, and we made goofy model poses as Mom snapped some candid shots with her phone. If prom itself was even half this fun, it was going to be an incredible night, date or no date.

We were interrupted by the doorbell.

"Aha, our special guests have arrived," my mom said as we traipsed back down the hallway to the living room—me wobbling in a new pair of three-inch heels. Mom opened the door to the apartment and revealed Dad and Ollie.

"*Sur*prise," Mom said in a singsong voice. "I thought you wouldn't mind having your boys along for dinner."

Dad was dressed handsomely in the Charlie Chaplin suit I'd borrowed at Halloween, while Ollie had on his green footie pajamas and a black clip-on bowtie.

"Who's the celebrity bombshell?" Dad said, eyeing my glamorous getup. "We'd better get some family photos, ASAP, before the little guy figures out how to get that tie off." Mom extended her arms to relieve him of my baby brother, who gurgled happily as she kissed him on the top of his blond head. The four of us posed while Margot snapped our picture. It occurred to me that there might not be anything very typical about our little brood, but the fact that we could all still get together as a family had to mean something, didn't it?

As much as I enjoyed our family dinner at the elegant, if past-its-prime French restaurant known for its crack-like chocolate mousse, I could barely eat a thing for fear of ruining my makeup. While Dad paid the check I began to get butterflies in my stomach in anticipation of the rest of the night. The only thing that would trump the humiliation factor of showing up without a date was being seen getting dropped off by my parents' station wagon in front of the Royal Plaza Hotel. I tactfully told Dad and Mom as much as we drove to the hotel, and instructed them on executing a stealth military-style drive-by at the corner. Ollie was already fast asleep in his car seat when I slammed the car door and made a break for the hotel entrance.

In the lobby, a blushing bellhop fell all over himself to give me directions to "Ballroom C," and although I still felt like a giraffe on roller skates in my high heels, I couldn't help but bask in my newfound revelation: I looked hot.

"Miss Kingston! Quite a change!" said Principal Schaeffer, who was positioned outside the ballroom along with some other faculty members, checking students in. "What, no camera around your neck tonight?" He shoved a ballpoint pen in my face and pointed out where I should John Hancock the "I won't drink" contract all attendees were forced to sign upon entry. He was either unaware or had turned a blind eye to the fact that most seniors were skilled in the art of smuggling booze. Even I knew sneaking the hard stuff into prom was as simple as washing out travel-sized plastic bottles of hand lotion or hair spray, then refilling them with vodka. *Voila*—instant shots to be downed in the bathroom. Adult chaperones inspecting purses were none the wiser. Didn't it strike them as odd that so many girls carried fifteen-pound tote bags with a week's worth of toiletry items instead of smaller clutches? Duh. I had no intention of getting trashed tonight, but I imagined dozens of my classmates had already hit the sauce.

Upon closer inspection of the grand ballroom, my first impression of the Prom Decorating Committee's handiwork was "amateur." There was a crudely adorned stage and a glittering disco-ball-topped dance floor, but the only other thing that disguised the room from being the site of tedious business conferences by day were reams upon reams of crepe paper and a large white banner that read, "Party Like It's 1399!!" in a medieval Gothic typeface. That, and the photography area: an archway of silver and white balloons, under which couples posed for cheezed-out portraits in front of a cardboard "stone" wall dotted with paint by numbers coats-of-arms. A silver monstrosity of a castle with bubble-gum pink turrets was shoved in the corner as if an afterthought. Gross. One more reason to be grateful I didn't have a date. Nevertheless, I was starting to feel just a tad conspicuous standing by myself in the middle of this cavernous room. I did a quick scan for Cat and company, but didn't see them anywhere.

"Skye Kingston?" I glanced over and saw Duff Wallace hanging his tux jacket on the back of a chair at an empty table. I smiled and gave a quick wave, not expecting that he'd actually motion for me to come over. I was half-surprised he even remembered me. "I barely recognized you!" he said, as I greeted him with a tentative hug. "You look *amazing!!*"

"Welcome home! How was Scotland?"

"If I never hear another set of bagpipes again in my life it'll be too soon."

"I can see where that might start to get a little grating over time."

"Like a duck being tortured. And did you know hamburgers over there are literally made out of *ham?*"

"Eww, gross! You're making that up."

"Okay, maybe," he said. "But whatever's in them, they are full-on nasty. And that's only for starters. They eat lamb guts and something called blood sausage over there. Can you tell I've lost weight?" I didn't know whether he wanted me to answer yes or no, and besides, he looked pretty much the same, so I grinned stupidly and said nothing. "So, who are you here with?"

"I came stag."

"No kidding." He looked genuinely surprised. I wasn't sure whether he really was interested in chatting with me or just being polite, but since I hadn't seen anyone else to glom onto, I decided to keep up the small talk for as long as he seemed willing.

"So . . . what's it like being back here now that you've seen the world?"

"To be honest, I have mixed emotions about all this." He motioned with his hand at the room in general, and I recognized a hint of glumness in his voice. "I never intended on missing my entire senior year here, and now that I'm back, well, everything seems different. Let's just say I'm not thrilled about the regime change . . . if you get my drift."

No sooner had the words escaped his mouth than Craig and Beth walked by, looking like they ought to be entering the Academy Awards surrounded by a team of bodyguards, publicists, paparazzi, and screaming fans. Beth was wearing a floor-length strapless black gown with a corseted bustier to maximize her cleavage. A side slit running the length of her skirt exposed nearly all of her left thigh. Her smoky eye-makeup and the black rose affixed to her blonde updo made her look like a tragically beautiful blood-sucking vampire. I didn't hear the catty remark she had just lobbed at Duff because I was too busy staring, trance-like, at Craig, who in turn couldn't take his eyes off me. In his black tuxedo suit, he looked taller and more dashing than I'd ever seen him. Bond-like, you might even say. By the time I snapped back to reality, Duff was issuing his former teammate a warning.

"Careful, bro," he said. "Don't reject the black widow or she might accuse you of date rape and get you shipped to Siberia. Hell, you're lucky to escape with your life. Just ask Duncan. *Oh wait.* He's not around to ask, *is he?*" Beth's eyes narrowed to mere slits.

"Our lawyers agreed that your reason for leaving town wouldn't be a topic of conversation," she said, seething.

"Oh that's right. You get to lie all you want and I don't get to say anything."

Beth scowled, but I noticed she didn't exactly argue his point. Craig was visibly unnerved. He jerked Beth away by the elbow and walked her to the corner of the room where they proceeded to have what looked like a heated discussion.

"Sorry about that, Skye," Duff said. "Those two are just long overdue for a karmic ass-kicking. Or maybe a not-so-karmic one."

"It's all Beth's doing," I said, grateful to have someone who seemed to perhaps know almost as much as I did about Beth's wicked ways.

"Oh, roger that," he said. "The ironic part is, only it's not so funny from my perspective: I wasn't even at the party where she claims I roofied her drink. She almost ruined my life with her lies. It was her word against mine. She's clearly mental, but MacKenzie? That dude's only looking out for number one."

"No, Craig's just collateral damage," I argued. "Beth's got this irrational hold over him, but he's not who you think he is—"

"Indecision *is* a decision," Duff said, with loads more wisdom than I would have expected from a jock. I couldn't help but venture deeper into this conversation.

"What's that you mentioned about Duncan?"

"Oh, nothing, really. He texted me a couple of days before he died saying she made a pathetic play for him. Totally unrelated to his death, of course, but still. It just proves what a skank she is."

Little did he know. Before I could reply, Kristy swooped in like a glittery lunatic to decree that Duff *must* join her on the dance floor. Just when I realized I was alone again, Kaya, Tess, and Cat descended upon me, laughing uproariously at something, as usual. Cat was wearing a drapey, off-the-shoulder minidress that matched the platinum streak in her hair. She looked punk-edgy without crossing the line into slutty. Tess wore an adorable teal fringed flapper dress with a white feather fascinator in her hair, hot pink fishnet stockings, and T-strap silver pumps. Kaya had an emerald green Grecian-style gown with braided fabric straps; a gorgeous white lily corsage was her only accessory.

"Girl, you look fierce! And oh my god—look Tess, she's not wearing her All-Stars for once," Kaya said, pointing at my shoes.

"I thought about it, but I figured I'd save 'em for a dressier occasion."

"Whatever. Come on, we saved you a place at our table."

The hours flew by as we danced up a sweaty, celebratory storm. My makeup had no doubt slid off my face, but I didn't care. In a few more weeks, my high school career would be behind me, and as I looked around this swirling room full of eighteen-year-olds attempting to look like sophisticated adults, I realized that all of these people would soon be *real* adults, mere footnotes on my life, never to be seen again. Even though I barely interacted with a quarter of the people in my graduating class, it felt bittersweet, as if I had some kinship of shared mutual experiences with every single person in the room.

A slow song interrupted a string of great music, prompting a changing of the guard on the dance floor. Singletons headed back to their tables, while starry-eyed couples walked to the center of the floor. As I weaved past a few tables, I encountered Lenny and Megan walking hand-in-hand toward me. Megan must have wisely talked him out of a coral-colored cummerbund to match her dress, but she hadn't managed to avoid the tacky LED-lit corsage that shone like a beacon on her wrist. Her face beamed even brighter.

"You guys look great," I said, giving them both hugs.

"See!" Lenny turned to Megan, with a startling intimacy in their body language. "I *told* you Skye was cool with it." Megan gave me a hesitant grin.

"I felt so awful about leaving you high and dry. I know how much you were looking forward to being Lenny's date."

"Don't give it a second thought," I said, rolling my eyes, inwardly, but still genuinely happy that this odd couple had found romance. "Who knew all your bickering had flirtatious undertones? I was more than happy to bow out, so no worries. Although I will say your date is looking good in that monkey suit."

Lenny grinned from ear to ear, just as Jillian bopped her way in our direction holding four plastic cups of sloshing red punch in her hands.

"A toast!" she said, pawning a drink off on each of us. "To the journalists of East Anchorage High! Wherever life takes us, may we continue to make headlines."

"Good ones, that is," Megan said.

"Cheers!" we said in unison. I desperately had to pee, so I excused myself and headed for the hallway in the direction of the lobby restroom. When I got there, I found Jenna waving her hands manically.

"What's the matter?"

"Oh, nothing, babe," she said with a smile. "Just air drying. A tree died for those paper towels, you know."

"Oh, yeah. Uh huh." I nodded. "Great dress!"

"*Sustain*able!" she said in a sing songy voice, twirling to show off a gown that looked at once both haute couture and Amish. "They're announcing King and Queen soon," she continued. "Do you think Beth's recent campaign to kiss the ass of every senior in school actually bought her any votes?"

"You never know. I've learned not to question the absolute power of cheerleaders. But I think she forgot to kiss mine, at least. Sorry, Jenna, my bladder is bursting."

"All right, go to it, girl. And here's for the one you didn't get from Beth!" She blew me a parting air kiss.

When I exited the ladies' room, I noticed Craig sitting alone in one of the brocade high-backed armchairs in the lobby. He'd ditched his tuxedo jacket and had undone his bowtie, which hung limply from his collar.

"Lose your way?" I casually remarked.

"That about sums it up." I stopped walking and returned to face him.

"Hey, they're coming to get you soon." He looked confused. Alarmed. "The grand coronation? The man who would be king? The first dance with your lovely queen and your adoring court and all that. They're announcing it any minute now."

"Yeah," he said with all the exuberance of someone waiting for his oil to be changed at Jiffy Lube. "You look stunning." He glanced at me with more purpose now. I sighed and sat down in the wingback chair next to his. Among this furniture, we looked like we should be ordering crumpets and tea from someone named Jeeves, not living it up at our high school prom.

"Everyone keeps saying that tonight," I said. "'You look great, I didn't recognize you' . . . blah, blah, blah."

"Well, it's true."

"So what? The three-hundred-and-sixty-four other days of the year I'm totally ugly? It's just a little makeup—it's not like some sorcerer magically reconfigured the molecular structure of my cells or something. It's a little insulting actually. Yesterday at school I was average, unremarkable, and today I'm a knockout? Whatever."

"Why do you always do that?"

"Do what?"

"Block any compliment that comes your way. I get the feeling it's easier for you, safer for you, to position yourself as the homely wallflower." My brain couldn't even begin to formulate a response to his statement, so I just stared at him, dumbfounded. "You've created this fortress around yourself," he continued, "this castle wall with a moat and a portcullis and a thick, ironclad door that says, 'Keep out.'" Damn, he just referenced a portcullis? Impressive. But he was wrong. Dead wrong.

"You hole yourself up in that darkroom," he said. "Hiding in there, hiding behind your camera—" How dare *he* accuse *me* of using avoidance tactics!

"Well, *you've* spent the last three years hiding any trace of our friendship!" I said, tears welling up in my eyes. He leaned back in his chair but said nothing. "I totally predicted it, too. I knew it would happen as soon as school started sophomore year."

"Go on."

"You pretended we were great friends for a few weeks, only to develop convenient memory loss when Beth came into the picture! If you had any idea what I've done for you—"

"I didn't pretend anything." Craig shook his head. "The way I remember it, you pulled a vanishing act, leaving me to fend for myself when school started. Do you know how hard it was for me to show up on the first day of school a few thousand miles away from my home and try to blend in? I felt like I had just landed on Mars. And where was my *only* friend—Skye—who I'd hoped would invite me to sit with her in the cafeteria or wait for me after school or swing by my locker to say 'hi'? Where was the *one person* I knew in a sea full of strangers? She was nowhere, and I mean *nowhere* to be found."

No. He was flipping this all around now. This wasn't how it happened. I thought back to my self-conscious sophomore self, avoiding eye contact with him, too shy to shout out to him when he was walking twenty paces ahead of me in the hallway . . . too sure he'd already have better plans if I asked him to a Friday night football game. Too intimidated by how cute he was, and too hard on myself to imagine his interest in me wouldn't wane. Was it really possible that my actions had played some role in the chasm that stretched out between us? Did my assumptions that he'd pull a "Skye who?" turn into a self-fulfilling prophecy?

"Here's a newsflash for you: in Illinois, I was a total reject," he continued. "I'm talking junior high bottomfeeder, the butt of everyone's jokes."

"*You?*"

"I was a scrawny piece of work, back then, and it was miserable. I wanted to die."

Craig? The official State Dork of Illinois? I didn't believe it.

"But then you moved here."

"Yeah, and met you, and things seemed to be looking up." There was a ringing sound behind us, and the elevator doors slid open to let out an older woman with a rolling suitcase.

"But those first few days of school, it was happening all over again," he said. "Ostracized by everyone, including you, for some reason. Not a soul to talk to. The Untouchable."

"But I didn't—" Before I could complete my thought, he interrupted.

"Then a miracle happened: Beth. A few weeks into the school year, it's like she adopted me or something. Next thing I know, all the sort of kids who had tortured me at my last school were slapping me on the back and laughing at my jokes, acting like I was God's gift. So hell yeah, I went with it, and I didn't look back. Maybe it turned out to be the wrong move, but I can't change it now. What's done is done."

I wanted to argue that Beth Morgan was hardly heaven-sent, or ask why he didn't just reach out to me when he thought I was ignoring him, but I didn't have a chance. Brett Sanders came running down the hall motioning for us.

"MacKenzie, get your ass in here. They're announcing Prom King!"

Brett hurried back to Ballroom C while Craig calmly extricated himself from his chair.

"Don't you get what I'm saying?" He turned and looked down at me. "It's all arbitrary. None of this means anything. One school's king is another school's target practice." He headed down the hall and left me sitting there, shell-shocked.

CHAPTER TWENTY-ONE

Double, Double, Toil and Trouble

BY THE TIME I'D RETURNED FROM THE BATHROOM again where I had attended to my tear-stained face, our senior class president, Selena Alvaro, was on stage with a microphone, holding an index card and looking authoritative. Everyone was gathered in a cluster around the dance floor, and I wormed my way through to where the girls were.

"Damn, I can't see anything," Kaya said, grumbling. "Why do I have to spend my life staring at people's shoulder blades?" In the middle of her fidgeting, her corsage dropped to the floor. She stooped down to pick it up. "Ow, dammit!"

"Are you okay?"

"Yeah, I just pricked my thumb on the pin," she said.

"Well don't get blood on your dress."

"Right." She popped her thumb in her mouth.

On a table next to Selena were a silver crown and a glittery tiara, as well as a pile of long-stemmed roses to be handed to the female members of the court. Near the dance floor, a quartet of cheerleaders huddled around Kristy, prepping her for what she hoped would be her big moment. If not for her sequined gown, and, well, the fact that she was a girl, she could have been a prizefighter about to enter the ring. I glanced around to find Beth. She was adjusting the rose in her hair, as if readying her coif for her coronation. Classmates of middling social status—a few of the

155

usual suck-ups—hovered near her. Beth turned to make sure that Craig was ready to roll. He was behind her, and oh god, he was staring at me again. What was with him? I quickly turned back around for some small talk with Cat to avoid his penetrating gaze.

"Did you ever see that movie, *Carrie*?" I said. "Maybe we should blow this joint."

"Oh, you're bad." She gave me a devilish grin. "But who needs a bucket of blood? Dump some water on Beth and it would do the trick. 'I'm melting! Melting!'" she screeched *à la* the Wicked Witch of the West. "*Oh, what a world!*"

"Hey, spread the word: afterparty at the Hurlyburly," Tess said, interrupting us.

"Oh great," mumbled Kaya, her thumb still in her mouth. "As if these people needed any more booze tonight."

With way more gravitas than was merited, Selena began calling up the members of the prom court. It was the typical beautiful-people brigade, although a popular indie hipster couple in moth-eaten vintage threads had broken into the ranks. Beth and Craig were finally called up to join the court, along with Kristy and Duff, who elicited a rousing cheer from the crowd. Kristy brightened at the warm reception for her boyfriend, assuming it augured well for her chances.

"And now, for the moment you've all been waiting for," Selena said. "It was a nailbiter, but we have a definitive winner for King and Queen. Drumroll, please." There were no drums to be found, so we all beat the palms of our hands on our thighs or stomped our feet for dramatic effect. "This year's Prom King and Queen of East Anchorage High . . . are. . . ." Wow, this girl was milking it. "Craig MacKenzie and Beth Morgan!"

Cheers erupted from the crowd, along with a few unmistakable boos. Beth tipped her head gracefully to receive the tiara and silently mouthed "Thank you," while gesturing to her fellow classmates like she was Eva Peron about to break into a rousing rendition of "Don't Cry For Me Argentina." Puh-leaze. Duff shrugged his shoulders good-naturedly and wrapped Kristy up in a comforting hug. Craig gave a weak smile and stumbled over to Selena to accept his crown.

"He looks trashed," said Cat.

"Mmm . . . I don't think so. I was just talking to him five minutes ago. But yeah, he does look kind of out of it."

"*SPEECH, SPEECH, SPEECH, SPEECH. . . .* " the crowd demanded. Selena shoved the microphone into Craig's hand. At the same time, Nick tossed a balled-up piece of fabric in Craig's direction. He caught and unfurled it, revealing Duncan's team jersey. His face went as white as his dress shirt.

"Dude, he looks like he's seen a ghost," Cat said. The crowd was still yelling for a speech, and Beth gave Craig an imploring look. "Say something!" her face all but screamed at him.

"Um, hey there," he said into the microphone. His deep voice seemed a little shaky. "What a night, huh?" A smattering of whoops and applause. "Wow, this is really an odd place to be standing right now. And why? Why am I up here? Because I score a lot of goals? Because I'm dating 'Sexy Sadie' over here?" he gestured to Beth, who looked confused and uncertain. Craig raised the fist holding Duncan's jersey. "Why am *I* still here and he's not?" Beth reached for the microphone in Craig's hand, but he yanked it back and took two steps away from her.

"Quit," he said. "You can't do that to me anymore. You're not going to silence me, you lying. . . ." Craig didn't finish the sentence, but I could hear gasps all around me. Beth looked around, a little panicked now, and the members of the prom court stood glancing at each other disconcertingly on the stage.

"What's he doing?" Kaya asked Tess.

"He's self-destructing."

"Or maybe he's finally taking control," I said. Craig was pacing the stage now, like a man possessed.

"I've been too silent for too long," he said, still hanging onto Duncan's jersey. Oh god, no. He wasn't going to spill his guts about Duncan's death right here and now? This was bad. This was looking *very* bad. "I want to thank all of you who voted for Beth and me. And yet it feels kind of ironic that I just won this popularity contest, because ask yourselves this: What kind of friend have I really been to you?" He paused, as if considering what to say next.

"You see," he said, "I've had only a couple of what I'd call 'true friends' at this school over the last three years, and I couldn't manage to hang onto either of them. I need to beg forgiveness from them both. One can't answer, unfortunately." He stared down at Duncan's jersey. "And I just hope it's not too late to let the other person know how I really feel."

At that moment, I wasn't aware of Cat or Tess or fury-faced Beth or anyone else in the room for that matter. It was just between Craig and me now. It was easy for him to lock eyes on me, because I stood taller than any of the other girls in the room. Whether anyone else realized that he was directing his comments to me was uncertain. "I sometimes think you understand me better than I understand myself. We wasted so much stupid time. Time I can never get back with you. Maybe I let my ambitions get the better of me. Maybe we both let our insecurities paralyze us. God knows I haven't been the easiest person to be around lately. . . . All I can say is, you've got to believe it when I say it was only ever you." Beth was in tears by now, humiliated. She stormed off the stage and headed for the lobby. Craig jumped down off the back of the stage and pushed his way through an exit door that led to the hotel kitchen.

"What was that all about!" Cat said, turning to me. "Was he talking to *you*!?!"

"I've got to go find him," I said.

"Oh no, we're not going to let you roam the hotel innards," Cat said. "Not without us, I mean." I rather wished my friends would let me handle this by myself, but I guess that was part of the tradeoff in having a posse: they actually looked out for you. The four of us headed off in the direction that Craig had gone. Since prom wasn't a catered event, the kitchen off the ballroom was not in use. Everything was neat, orderly, and quiet. No hotel employees were anywhere in sight. But neither was Craig. An unlit stairwell led off the kitchen.

"Could he have gone down here?" Kaya wondered.

"It's worth a try." In her flapper-era getup, Tess looked like she was venturing into a secret speakeasy as she led us down the flight of stairs. We made our way through a maze of dim hallways, past the laundry room, the cleaning crew's station, and then down another flight of stairs.

"I wish we had a flashlight," said Cat. At the end of a long dark hallway, I finally saw something reflect what little ambient light was available. Craig was sitting, back to the wall, dangling the crown from his fingers between his bent knees. We must have been somewhere directly under the ballroom, because I could hear the faint sound of music again from up above.

"It's okay, girls, you can leave us," I said, squatting to be on Craig's level.

"No, they should stay," Craig said. The girls stood there looking awkward, as if they'd really rather give us our privacy. Craig held up the crown and glanced at it from underneath, as if it were a scientific specimen. "Isn't it funny, how you guys called it from the beginning?"

"I don't follow," said Kaya.

"You said I'd be king. Or I guess it was that mask you had me try on. 'A warrior king,' isn't that what you said, Cat?" Nobody responded. "But you also warned me it could mean death. That part ended up being true, too."

"Craig, really . . . I mean, I don't think," Cat said, trailing off.

"Oh believe me, I'm not one to buy into all that witchcraft nonsense," he hastened to add.

"I wouldn't call it witchcraft," I said quietly.

"Still, there's no denying that it was right. So ladies. . . ." Craig looked up at my friends. "What other prophecies do you have up your sleeves?"

"Craig," I said, soothingly, as Tess shot me a concerned glance. "It's all behind you now."

"That's right," Cat said, unaware of what I was really referring to. "We've practically graduated. That's all she wrote, man. Ten-four, onward and upward, the best is yet to come."

"So you're telling me I'm off the hook?"

"Of course. It's all good!"

"I'm out of the woods?"

"You don't have to worry about the woods, you don't have to worry about the forest, you don't have to worry about a single tree for that matter," said Kaya cheerfully.

"God, it would be nice if I could believe that," he said, sighing. I took his hand in mine and gave it a squeeze.

"Tess, Cat, weren't we supposed to go get our prom favors before they all ran out?" Kaya said.

"Oh right. I think they're picture frames. Skye, do you want us to grab you one?"

"That would be terrific," I said, giving my girls a grateful look.

"I like them," Craig said when they rounded the corner. He was still grasping my hand. The music coming from upstairs was just the faintest noise now, as I sat back against the wall next to him and nestled my shoulder behind his. He perched his crown on my head.

"Was I a total idiot up there?"

"Well, the most memorable kings were the crazy ones. You know: Mad King George. . . ."

"Caligula. . . ."

"Well, he was an emperor. . . ."

"What," Craig said, teasingly. "Are you saying I couldn't be emperor if I wanted to?"

"Hey, sure. Like I've told you before, you control your own destiny."

"Yeah, well, this probably sounds nuts, but I think I took my first step toward controlling my own destiny tonight."

"I think so, too." We sat in silence for a moment, each gripping the other's hand. I was glad it was dark, because I still felt awkward and self-conscious, especially after everything Craig had said to me tonight.

"So, I'll say it again: You look amazing."

"Thanks."

"Right answer."

"Did you really mean what you just said up there?"

"Yes . . . and so much more. Three years too late, I guess."

"It's never too late."

"Sometimes it is," he said. "But I'm glad it's not too late in this case." He looked over at me, and even though I could barely see him, I flushed red, averting my gaze. The intensity of the moment was too overwhelming for me. Every cell in my body felt alive with possibility.

"There's one thing I still haven't gotten, though," he said thoughtfully after a few minutes.

"What's that?"

"A dance with you." He stood up and pulled me to standing along with him. The music was barely audible, but there was enough for us to sway to in this long, dark hallway. It was so dark, in fact, that I couldn't look into his eyes, but I knew his lips hovered a few inches from mine. Being tall had its advantages, I realized. His long hands were clasped on my lower back and my cool fingers grazed the back of his warm neck. I was still the eighteen-year-old dork who'd never been kissed, but having spent the last four years worrying about the technical logistics of locking lips with a boy—where to stick my nose, what to do with my tongue, how to angle my mouth—it now seemed so obvious. In that perfect moment, your brain no longer factors into the equation. And neither do words.

CHAPTER TWENTY-TWO

Drink, Sir, Is a Great Provoker

IF I COULD HAVE REMAINED IN THAT DARK UNDER-BELLY of the hotel, I think I would have been content to hide away there with Craig forever. But of course, that was impossible. I didn't know what to expect when he and I headed back up those two flights of stairs. Would re-emerging to the surface of the earth fling us back in time, as if our stolen kiss had never happened? Would Craig and I return to our respective social circles, keeping up the façade that we'd carefully constructed over the past three years? As we ascended step by step, Craig's hand gripped mine tightly, but I kept waiting for him to release my grasp once we came back into contact with civilization. Because what would everyone say if they found us paired-off? It would likely cause a rip in the fabric of the space-time continuum or at least burn the retinas of disbelieving classmates. In any case, I was certain that Beth could quite feasibly morph into a giant prehistoric monster and swallow me whole.

To my surprise, and to the surprise of the growing throngs of butterflies amassing in my stomach, Craig kept my hand firmly in his. He apparently wasn't concerned about public perception. Not that we caused much of a stir. The ballroom was emptying out, and the deejay was packing up his equipment as we glanced around at the few people who were still lingering.

"Guess everyone's off to the afterparty," I said.

"Wanna go?"

"With you?"

"Yeah, with me, knucklehead. Who else?"

"But what about Beth?" Craig sighed ruefully and acknowledged that I had a point.

"She's not my favorite person right now, but I'd better try to find her." Figures. Here was the part where he went groveling after his real girlfriend and I was left feeling like a schmuck as we went our separate ways after all. But instead, Craig tightened his grasp on my hand as we approached a few stragglers. "Anybody seen Beth around?"

"Lose a member of your harem?" said class comedian Tyler Babcock, who eyed Craig and me with some amusement. "Our dear Queen of Tarts was last seen out front, ordering your limo driver to put the pedal to the metal. That lady did not look happy. Think it's possible to actually die of embarrassment?"

Craig looked back at me warily, as if to say yikes.

"That means I'm officially rideless. How are you guys getting to the Hurlyburly?" he asked Tyler.

"We're going with Stefani and his lady."

"Got room for two more?"

"No, but when did that ever stop you?"

• • •

You always hear on the news about teens killed in car crashes and wonder why the idiots weren't wearing seatbelts. As I crouched to keep my head from hitting the ceiling of Dan Stefani's Subaru station wagon, I was one of those idiots. I hoped that Craig's arm, currently hooked around my waist, was strong enough to keep me from being propelled through the windshield in the event of an accident. I could die, both literally and figuratively. Figuratively, because I couldn't believe I was sitting on Craig's lap right now.

Granted, there were four other couples crammed into the car—not exactly the most romantic of interludes, but still, I felt downright punchy with exhilaration. This was the best night of my life.

"Five-O, keep it low!" yelled Dan as we went through an intersection. Everyone tried to duck so as to not be seen by the squad car in the oncoming lane. At least I could be certain Dan was sober—his family was über-Christian. I don't think the guy would even take an aspirin if his life depended on it.

Behind us in the hatchback, Trista Sarvak and Matt Lackey were swapping spit like gangbusters. My face hovered directly above Craig's in my contorted position on his lap, but I'd have been way too embarrassed to kiss him with all these other people around despite the fact that I really wanted to—how could people be so okay with public displays of affection?

"How much do you think the tux place will charge me for losing my jacket?" Craig said to no one in particular. Before leaving the hotel, we looked everywhere for his coat but couldn't find it. Another guy must have swiped his by mistake.

"Like your dad would even notice an extra charge to his gold card," said fellow jock, Kevin Wunar, who was crammed with his girlfriend, Stacey, on the far side of the back seat.

"Good point. Yo, Stefani—open the sunroof for a second," Craig said. When the glass window slid all the way back, he stuck his flimsy crown out the roof and let it go flying in the wind.

"Dude! Sweeeeet!" said Matt, coming up for air from Trista's face to watch the crown bounce along the road behind us. It finally spiraled to a stop in someone's front yard. At the same time, I felt Craig pinch me on the behind.

"Hey!" I laughed and shifted in my seat across his thighs. He pursed his lips in a tight smile, an adorable, "Who me?" look on his face. Fact was, I needed to be pinched. This all seemed totally surreal. And yet one growing concern continued to gnaw at me. Yes, all my hopes concerning Craig were beginning to manifest before my very eyes. Maybe he'd dump Beth . . . but then what? I was fairly certain, after all, that I was in love with a murder suspect. Whether it was negligent homicide or manslaughter or just a tragic, terrible accident, it was still an issue. This wasn't just a small character flaw, like being a bad tipper or never arriving places on time. This was major.

With Craig's strong hand resting solidly on my knee, I decided that, for tonight at least, I would allow myself some selective amnesia. At some point, yes, we'd need to have *that* conversation, but we didn't need to have it tonight. If Beth got to be Prom Queen, then I could certainly be Queen of Denial.

The parking lot at the bar was crowded, as usual, so we parked on a nearby side street and hoofed it. Craig carried me for the last block once he noticed that I wasn't the most agile pedestrian in high heels.

Inside, the bar was packed. I followed Craig, whose arm reached back behind him, holding mine, while he muscled his way through the crowd. I was a little terrified about coming face to face with Beth. It was bad enough having all the rubberneckers in the room checking out the fact that Craig had showed up with me. Fortunately, I didn't spy her anywhere in the crowd.

As we inched our way parallel to the bar, I noticed that all the over-forty crew had wisely vacated the joint. The line for ordering drinks was at least three-feet deep, but Craig was tall enough that he caught Easy's eye straight away.

"Hey, Ace," Craig said, as familiar as if he and Easy spent time bivouacked in the jungles of Vietnam together. "Can we get a pitcher of Coke and some glasses?"

Behind me, Matt Lackey snickered. "Yeah, *Coke*," he emphasized, raising his fingers to make air quotes. "With a little something else, if you know what I mean."

Easy winked back at Matt and continued hustling behind the bar. Through the crowd to my left, I saw Kaya, Tess, and Cat huddled in a corner with some of the student council kids. Cat threw me a subtle "thumbs up" at hip level, raising her eyebrows to convey that she was impressed. Kaya and Tess smiled and waved. I gave them the "one second" signal, figuring I'd mosey in their direction to fill them in once Craig and I had staked out some standing room of our own. The room was deafening as what amounted to my entire senior class continued to up the decibel level with every passing minute. Glancing back toward the entrance, I saw a steady stream of people filing in the door. Craig finally claimed some territory for us on the far side of the bar, but it was tight. He backed up to make a little more room for our carload, inadvertently bumping his elbow into the back of someone who was belly-up to the bar. Duff slowly swiveled around on his bar stool.

"You need to back it up. Now," he said, his tone ominous.

"Sorry man." Craig raised his hands in surrender. Duff furrowed his brow and turned back toward the bar. Easy hoisted over a pitcher of Coke and a stack of plastic cups. Craig passed the cups out and started pouring.

"None for me," I said when he handed one to me. He shrugged and passed it on. Brett Sanders, now wearing his bowtie around his forehead, crammed his way in between Craig and me. He looked like Rambo, and his cheeks were flushed. I wondered exactly how over-the-legal-limit his blood alcohol level was. It would have been nice to just have Craig to myself, without the mob scene. It's not like I really had much to say to any of his circle, after all. He must have sensed, by my silence, what I was thinking, because he sidled behind Brett back to my side.

"What's up, girl," he said, taking a sip of his spiked Coke. "Can you believe we're graduating in a few weeks?"

"No, it's so crazy."

"Hey, so what are you doing next year anyway?"

"USC."

"Wait. What?!?"

"USC," I repeated over the din. Next to Craig, a drunken Brett got to gesticulating so wildly that he bumped Craig's elbow. Some of his drink sloshed out of his glass, landing, unfortunately, on Duff's back. His soaking shoulders cringed their way up to his ears and he slowly turned around. A silence fanned out across the restaurant as people realized what had just happened.

"Duff, oh my god, I am so sorry." Craig reached over the bar for some napkins but Duff didn't seem interested in having his back dabbed down.

"It's totally my fault, bro," said Brett.

"I don't think so." Duff glowered, staring down Craig. "I told you before I was about sick of your bullshit, MacKenzie. You *had* to go push your luck, didn't you? It's *on* now." The tightly packed crowd backed up to give the two guys some elbow room, as it seemed clear this wasn't going to end well. Duff inched closer to Craig, looking pissed off and menacing.

"Duff, will you just chill?" Craig asked. "It was an accident, man . . . spill something on me if it would make you feel better. You don't have to get all aggro."

"I probably don't," Duff said, "But this is sure going to make me feel a hell of a lot better—"

Craig didn't even have time to duck. It took only one well-placed punch from Duff to drop him instantly to the floor. I shrieked, along with most of the girls in the room while the guys all chimed in with "FIGHT, FIGHT, FIGHT. . . !"

Craig stumbled to his feet. There was a gash above his left eye, which was already starting to swell. A line of blood trickled down his temple. He put both arms up in a gesture of peace, but when Duff lunged at him again, Craig grabbed him by the waist and pushed his back against the bar. Glasses toppled as Easy hurdled over the bar and tried to separate them. The crowd was still going nuts while Craig and Duff struggled to overpower each other. A waitress tried spraying them with the nozzle she used to fill Coke glasses, but to little avail. Duff pushed Craig back down on the ground and pounded his face with two more punches before Easy finally managed to pull him off.

By this time, a bouncer who'd been standing at the entrance barreled through and began ordering everyone out. Easy roughly ushered Duff toward the exit. "I'm glad Duncan's not around to see what you've become!" Duff yelled back at Craig before disappearing out the door.

I rushed and knelt by Craig's side. His face was still wet with Coke, which was now mixing with rivulets of blood. He looked up at me and groaned before blacking out completely.

CHAPTER TWENTY-THREE

The Patient Must Minister to Himself

IT WAS MUCH QUIETER IN THE RESTAURANT when Easy finally knelt down next to me with what looked like a tackle box. Craig was just beginning to come to, and I stroked his arm as Easy dug through his kit. He brought forth a brown bottle of hydrogen peroxide, but the fact that he was using his nicotine-stained teeth to open a cellophane package of gauze pads seemed a bit paradoxical in terms of sterility.

"Now don't you go movin' round, boy," he said when Craig lifted his head in a woozy attempt to look up. Easy dabbed at the gashes on Craig's face with the peroxide-soaked pads, making Craig wince with pain.

"Oh it hurts?" the old codger said with more than a hint of sarcasm. "And serves you right, too, starting a donnybrook like that in my bar." Craig and I exchanged "huh?" glances with each other as Easy rooted around in his tackle box some more.

"This old gal doesn't get much attention these days," he continued, patting the box like it was a trusted hunting dog. "But she's seen far worse than your scratches, I daresay." I noticed on the side of the box a medical insignia; an eagle-winged cross with two serpents. I randomly remembered my mom once called it a caduceus, or something like that. A perfectly useless *Jeopardy* fact. Easy must have noticed me looking at it because he proudly said, "That's right—combat medic in the First Battalion, Eighth

Cavalry. This is child's play compared to the things I patched up in 'Nam."

Craig clearly wasn't in the position to say much, so I figured it was up to me to make polite small talk.

"Sorry about all the craziness," I said. Two waitresses and the beefy bouncer were clearing dishes off the tables and starting to wipe them down.

"Why is it that you preppy high school kids always manage to make the Hells Angels look like stalwarts of civility?" Easy wondered. "You come in here all fancy-like with your dresses and penguin suits and next thing I know I'm mopping blood off the floor."

Easy started using his teeth again to cut medical tape. He'd made a gauze bandage that he was now affixing to Craig's forehead.

"Well," I countered tactfully, "alcohol is probably a factor."

"That's why I don't serve minors."

"Oh riiigght." I assumed he was being facetious.

"I figure I can keep the lot of you safe if you think you're drinking here."

"If we *think*?"

"I wouldn't risk my liquor license and everything I've worked thirty years for to help a bunch of adolescents get sauced."

"But I thought. . . ."

"Of course you did. And so does everyone else. In the medical profession, you might call it the 'placebo effect.' Apparently all you young geniuses who have the computer so figured out can't tell the difference between whisky and almond syrup."

"Almond syrup? *That's* what you spike the drinks with?'" I felt a smile inch across my face.

"Tastes just unusual enough to convince you that your Cokes have been turned into cocktails."

"Oh, brother." Craig had finally joined the conversation. He was propped up on his elbows now, his hair still damp with soda.

"I've left here some nights thinking I was bombed out of my mind. Are you for real?"

"It was all in your noggin," Easy said, knocking his own knuckles against his salt-and-pepper scalp. "Let's just say I've earned a pretty good profit margin off almond sodas in my day. But let's keep this all our little secret."

Secret-keepers? He had picked two of the best. Craig was drinking from a tumbler of water that a waitress had handed him when I glanced around the deserted bar, wondering how we were supposed to get home. I was about to ask Easy to call us a cab when the front door of the establishment burst open. In strode Craig's barrel-chested dad, wearing khaki pants and a red-and-black flannel hunting jacket. With his silver hair and chiseled features, he looked distinguished, but also jerky. His face made it clear this was not a pleasure call.

"Dad!" Craig said, practically gasping.

"Here you are. Why are you hanging out in a bar, alone, at two o'clock in the morning? And what's with your face?" Easy glanced up from drying his glasses but said nothing.

"Dad, it was after prom. Everyone just left. We were just about to head home ourselves, but I knocked my head—"

"*WE??*" Mr. MacKenzie snorted cynically and glanced at me. "And who is *WE?*"

"This is Skye. She's a friend, Dad. I've told you about her before."

"I don't want to hear about your little friend. What I want to know is why your girlfriend turned up on my doorstep bawling her eyes out about an hour ago."

"I tried to find her! She took off in the limo and I figured she was pissed off at me—"

"What kind of jerk-off abandons his prom date in the middle of the night? Is that the kind of man I raised you to be? While your mother and I were trying to talk that pretty little girl of yours down off a ledge, you were out here making moves on some other unsuspecting young hussy?"

"Dad. STOP."

"You're coming home. NOW. Get in the goddamned car."

"I can't leave Skye here."

"You left another girl tonight . . . you can do it again. Now get in the car before I kick your ass six ways to Sunday."

"Skye. . . ." Craig looked at me, pleadingly and apologetic.

"I can take a cab. It's fine. *Really.*"

"I'll call you." He followed his dad, dejectedly, out the front door. I heard the sound of a truck engine rev and the tires squealed as they careened out of the parking lot. The two exhausted-looking waitresses gave their boss pecks on the cheek before slinging purses over their shoulders and heading out the rear exit. Easy glanced at me sympathetically.

"Looks like you could use a *real* drink."

"Nah. . . ." I sighed, but I took a seat at one of the bar stools anyway. Elbows on the bar, my chin in my hands, I looked at him glumly as he emptied out the cash drawer on the register and began separating the bills into piles.

"Craig's a good kid," he said offhandedly. I muttered my assent. "His dad comes in here every now and then. Bit of a hardass, that one." I nodded again. "But he brags about his kid every time he's in here. Can't get the man to shut up."

I found that seriously hard to believe, which Easy must have judged from my facial expression because he changed the subject.

"So, how was the ball, Cinderella?"

"Okay . . . but I think my carriage has officially turned back into a pumpkin. Speaking of, would you mind calling me a taxi?"

"My pleasure." While Easy was on the phone with a cab company, I checked myself out in the mirrored wall behind the shelves of liquor. Margot and my mom had done a good job. My makeup was surprisingly still mostly in place and the curls in my hair hadn't completely collapsed yet.

Easy turned back around, stuffing his stack of bills into a leather envelope.

"You got enough cash to pay the driver?" he asked, paternally.

"Yeah." I patted my satin clutch purse. He continued fussing around with accoutrements behind the bar before circling his way back to me.

"So . . . if you were here with the MacKenzie boy, then what's this about him having a girlfriend? Is that the bossy little blonde I've seen him with?"

"Yeah, that is she. It's a long story."

"Well now, I'm staying put here till your cab comes, so enlighten me."

"I get the sense things are over between them as of tonight. It was long overdue. The problem is, she's always had it out for me, and now that Craig and I are together. . . ."

"Let me guess: 'Hell hath no fury like a woman scorned.'"

"Bingo."

"Aww, I wouldn't pay her too much mind. Seems to me that girl is a good two feet shorter than you. I think you could take her."

"I hope it doesn't come to that!" I laughed nervously. "I mean, *jeez!*"

"I never underestimate the petty squabbles of the so-called weaker sex. Some of the catfights we've had in here could rival the medieval berserkers. Guys can be belligerent, but women? They can be downright evil."

"Uh, you're not making me feel any better."

"Right. Sorry."

Easy continued cleaning up behind the bar as I sat with my chin in my hand, wondering what Beth would say to me Monday at school. Eventually, my cell started to vibrate in my clutch, so I reached to grab it just as the telephone behind the bar started to ring. I glanced at a text message from Craig.

Skye. Soooo sorry. Meet me at Regent asap . . . will explain l8ter.

"Your cab's here," Easy announced.

"Thanks," I said, smiling. "Craig just texted. Sounds like he's okay."

"That was fast," Easy said. "His dad must have been burning rubber."

"He might have texted from the car."

"Oh . . . you're probably right. You kids and your infernal cell phones."

"Thanks for everything. I'll see you around."

"Ten-four, doll." When I slid in the back seat of the taxi, my heart was racing again. I instructed the cabbie to drive me to the Regent Theater, wondering how and why Craig would want to meet up with me there.

CHAPTER TWENTY-FOUR

Is This a Dagger
Which I See Before Me?

"YOU SURE YOU WANT TO BE DROPPED OFF HERE, GIRLIE?" I handed the grizzled cabbie a tenner and hopped out onto the still-wet, abandoned street. "It's getting late," he said.

"Yeah, it's fine. I'm meeting someone."

"If you say so." He shrugged.

I still hadn't gotten the knack of wearing heels and had to catch my balance as I leapt over a puddle and onto the sidewalk. It was well after two a.m. when the yellow cab pulled away from the curb, so I was surprised to see the bright pink neon of the Regent sign reflected in the pavement. It usually closed at midnight. I wished I'd brought along my camera. The empty street and the theater would've made for a gorgeous shot. They must be hosting a special midnight showing, I mused. If so, why did Craig want me to meet him here? Though I guess if we had a place that was "ours," this was it. Was it his way of attempting a symbolic fresh start at the place where it had all begun? I pulled my wrap closer around me. It was a romantic idea, but a little late to be continuing where we'd left off in the hotel basement earlier that night. Just thinking about it made my heart thump wildly in my chest.

I walked over to the glass door and peered inside. All the lights were on, but I didn't see anyone working at the counter. Maybe they'd simply forgotten to turn the sign off? I pulled at the door, half expecting it not to open, but it did, and so I walked into the brightly lit but quiet lobby.

"Craig," I said, my voice echoing back as if from the bottom of a well. The doors leading into the screening room were closed, but I could hear the sound of a movie playing inside, so I slipped in quietly and shut the door carefully behind me so as not to disturb the other filmgoers. Up on the screen, I recognized the face of James Dean. I'd never seen this film, but based on the iconic red jacket and white T-shirt he wore, I figured it must be the teen tragedy, *Rebel Without a Cause*.

I peered into the darkened theater and waited for my eyes to adjust to the darkness. There didn't seem to be anyone here, but then I had the strange sensation that I wasn't alone . . . someone was standing very close to me in the dark. I knew instinctively that it wasn't Craig, and I took a step back and reached my hand out, feeling for the door behind me. "Who's there?" I asked.

"Wait," said an assertive female voice from the dark. "Don't leave." Thank god; it was only Beth. Wow, I thought. Her uncle is making her clean the place on prom night? That's harsh. But then another thought occurred to me: How awkward would this be once Craig showed up to meet me? Granted, he would need to have it out with her at some point, but tonight didn't seem like the most opportune moment to let her know she was officially being replaced by yours truly. Easy was right: Hell hath no fury like a woman scorned, and when that woman was Beth Morgan, look out. Maybe if I thought quickly, I could head him off before they ran into each other. But how was I supposed to explain to her what I was doing here in the first place?

As Beth drew closer I realized she was still wearing her prom dress, though it was ripped at the bottom, and Craig's tuxedo jacket was draped around her thin shoulders. Of course! It hadn't occurred to us that Beth might have taken the coat with her when she left the dance like a bat out of hell. Her face was streaked with tears and makeup and glowed pale and ghostlike from the dark. With her black gown blending in with the dark of the theater, her head—still topped with the garish crown—looked eerily unattached to her body. On-screen, James Dean's character was crying to his parents: *We're all involved, Mom! A boy was killed! I don't see how we can get out of that by pretending it didn't happen!*

"Beth! I didn't realize you'd be—"

"Don't talk. You've done quite enough already tonight, as it is." She reached up to her head and pulled off the tiara. Part of her blonde hair snagged on the plastic comb, forcing her to wrench it off her head violently.

"May as well give this to you, too," she said. "You've taken everything else from me, after all."

"I'm not sure what you—"

"I said, *DON'T TALK!*" she screamed. Her eyes could have burned holes through my skull the way she was looking at me. She grabbed my hand forcefully and pulled me along behind her toward the movie screen. Her hand felt cold and clammy against mine and I fought the urge to pull away, knowing it would only anger her even more. My skin crawled with something akin to instinctual fear, but I pushed it down. Beth could be intimidating, but she wasn't anything I couldn't handle.

Standing by the second row of seats, Beth now pointed to the seat closest to us. Draped over it was her prized cheerleading jacket. "You saw it, didn't you?" she said. "You know it's there." I knew she was talking about the spot on the jacket. This was getting weirder by the minute. On-screen, the actors' faces looked ten-feet high and were, from this angle, eerily distorted. "The blood." She was almost hissing now. "You see it, too! I know you do."

"Beth, what's going on?" I asked, trying to remain calm. I was relieved when she let go of my hand and I quickly folded my arms against my chest. Alone with Beth in a darkened movie theater, the last thing I wanted to talk about was the damning speck of blood on her jacket. Just thinking about Beth's role in Duncan's death made my own blood boil, but I feigned ignorance.

"You know *exactly* what's going on," she said, ignoring my dumbfounded stares. "You've had it out for me from the beginning."

"But I didn't!"

"Right. This is *all* because of you. You loathed me for taking Craig away from you, and you wanted payback. You were going to steal Craig back from me."

"What?!"

"I knew it. I knew it by the way he looked at you, by the way he talked about you . . . and Duff and Duncan didn't want me, either. No one wanted me." She broke down into heart-wrenching sobs and I couldn't help but feel pity for her. She was obviously still having some psychological issues.

"Beth, it's okay," I said, reaching over to pat her awkwardly on the shoulder.

"Don't touch me," she said, jerking her arm away. She pointed again at the cheerleading jacket. "This is your fault. I never would've went for Duncan if I hadn't thought Craig would leave me. I had to take drastic measures."

"So it's true?" I asked, trying to keep my voice ambivalent. "You made a pass at Duncan?"

"So what?" she said. "Craig was cheating on *me* . . . if not physically, at least mentally."

"Craig never cheated on you," I said. Still, Craig's acceptance speech earlier tonight was proof enough, in Beth's mind, that she was right all along. I couldn't exactly deny that—nor did I want to, if truth be told. But it was no crime.

"It's all your fault," she repeated again. "You made me do it."

"But—I don't understand."

"Once I saw the way Craig was looking at you at the party that night, I knew I was losing him. I had to give him a reason not to leave me."

"How can you blame me?" I was almost shouting. "You're the reason Duncan didn't survive. Why didn't you let someone know what happened right away? Why did you make Craig promise not to tell anyone?"

"You knew all along." Her eyes narrowed into ferocious slits. "Were you spying on us? Or let me guess: your little Craigiepoo made you a heartfelt confession? How much did he tell you?"

"Craig didn't tell me anything."

"Yeah, well he doesn't have to live with what I have to live with. I'm the one who—" she stopped herself. "But it doesn't matter."

"How can you say that?!" I said. "If you'd been honest that night, someone could have gotten to Duncan. He was still—"

"Alive? Craig and I both saw him go in that icy water. There was no way we could have known he'd somehow manage to pull himself out. He was as good as dead when we left him."

"And it was your idea not to tell anyone. I heard everything when you were standing by the Jeep that night."

"It was the only way."

"No. I'm . . . I'm going to go get help," I said, my teeth chattering as if I were there in the snow that dark night with Duncan. Just as I started to turn away, I froze. In her right hand, which peeked from beneath Craig's jacket, something shimmered. She turned toward me and I registered instantly the steel blade of the knife in her hand.

"Beth, don't," I begged as I backed away, holding my hands in front of me. "You're not thinking straight."

"If anyone is to blame for Duncan's death, it's you," she said, inching closer. "I wouldn't have had to lie to Craig. He and Duncan wouldn't have fought. Duncan wouldn't have fallen through the ice." She looked like a zombie. And what did she mean by "I wouldn't have had to lie to Craig?" Was she talking about lying to the police?

I stumbled over myself as I tried to back away from her. These *damn* heels! She grabbed my arm. I could barely tear my eyes from the glint of the knife in her other hand. When I looked up, Beth's stare was almost vacant.

"Beth, you don't want to do this," I said, sobs choking my words. "I'm not going to say anything to anyone. Please. Don't!" I closed my eyes and tried to brace for the impending pain as she raised her arm over her head. I imagined her lunging toward me, and the next thing I knew I'd fallen to the ground, my head hitting the concrete floor. Lights blinded me and I shut my eyelids tight, afraid to open them. I could hear Beth's rasping sobs. And then I heard another voice.

"Skye! Are you okay?" I opened my eyes and saw Craig kneeling next to me, frantic. Easy had both of his burly arms wrapped around Beth, and the knife was about two feet away on the floor. Beth was squirming against Easy's grasp. I tried to sit up but I felt too dizzy and swooned against Craig. When I could open my eyes again, I glanced back at Easy. Beth now looked like an exhausted, limp ragdoll in his arms. She was weeping incessantly and her speech was incoherent.

"Is she okay?" I asked him, putting my hand up to touch the knot on my head. "What are you two doing here?"

"Ray, your cabbie, swung back by the Hurlyburly," Easy answered. "Said he'd dropped you here, and thought it seemed fishy. Then Craig called me from home wondering if he'd left his phone at the bar. Realized he couldn't have sent you that message."

"So, who. . . ?" I trailed off, realizing it must have been Beth who'd texted me, pretending to be Craig. "I thought she was you."

"I left my phone in the pocket of my tux coat," Craig said, stroking my forehead lightly. "I bolted over here as soon as I got off the phone with Easy."

"Even though I *told* you to sit tight and let *me* handle the situation," Easy said, grumbling.

"Now what do we do?" Craig looked at Easy for help, indicating Beth with a nod of his head.

"It's up to Skye," he answered. "Do you want to press charges?"

I thought about it for a second. She'd almost killed me. She'd known Duncan was still alive and had left him to die in the wilderness. But if I did turn her over to the police and Beth told her story, Craig would probably be arrested, too. And none of this would bring back Duncan. I thought about campouts and sing-alongs with Beth when we were both in Brownies together as little girls. Sure, she had changed plenty since then, but she was still that same girl, and I couldn't help but pity her, strange as it sounds. I decided I'd take my chances rather than put Craig in jeopardy.

"No," I shook my head slowly. "But she needs help."

"Her dad's an old buddy of mine. I'll give him a call to get over here . . . make sure he understands that she needs to see a professional," Easy said. "I've seen this kind of thing before. She's in shock right now. You two should take off before she comes out of this and realizes what happened."

Craig helped me up and we walked out into the lobby. He pulled me close, looking into my eyes, and said, "I'm so sorry this happened to you. I didn't handle any of it well. I feel responsible."

"There's been enough blame thrown around tonight," I said, wondering how much, if anything, he and Easy had overheard before Beth got all dagger-happy on me. He looked at me questioningly and I decided they hadn't heard much.

"You might have handled it better," I admitted, squeezing his hand. "The public declaration probably wasn't your best idea ever, but I appreciate the gesture."

"I don't know what I would've done if anything had happened to you," he said pulling me to him. Who cares if Beth almost killed me tonight, I thought. At least now I could die happy.

CHAPTER TWENTY-FIVE

Me Thought the Wood Began to Move

DUNCAN WASN'T THE ONLY ONE FATED TO DIE my senior year at East Anchorage High. It was a sunny afternoon, one of our last days of the school calendar, and as a symbolic nod to the future, Old Burny was about to meet its maker. The entire student body gathered on the green grassy quad just after lunch to bid the ancient tree farewell. On a raised dais, Principal Schaeffer, the city's school superintendent, and various other local dignitaries sat on folding chairs in front of a microphoned podium, including Edward Shaw, Duncan Shaw's father, who was a member of the school board. I only knew his face from seeing him at Duncan's memorial service in the gym last fall. It seemed ironic that we were now holding a similar ceremony for a tree, of all things. Off to the left, an enormous yellow Caterpillar backhoe waited like a looming dinosaur, eager to get this show on the road.

The tree would be cut down in a few days, and the quad, in its entirety, would be demolished as part of grand plans for an impressive new addition to the school. The renovation had been seriously hyped for most of my four years here, but only recently were the architectural plans revealed in the *Daily News*, showing where a brand new state-of-the-art theater and auditorium would be built on the site of the current parking lot. The quad would be paved over for the new parking lot, and Old Burny—who had toughed out a ravaging wildfire more than a century ago, not to mention having endured bitter winters and plenty of teenage graffiti ever since—would be reduced to kindling.

As class president, Selena Alvaro delivered what she thought was a fitting tribute, reading from Shel Silverstein's *The Giving Tree* (as if that would somehow make us all less culpable for tree murder). I glanced around expecting to find an outraged Jenna, but she was strangely keeping a low profile. In mourning, I suspected.

"That was just depressing," said Craig at Selena's conclusion of the book. "I always preferred *Where the Sidewalk Ends*."

"Did you know Shel Silverstein wrote 'A Boy Named Sue?'" Kaya leaned in and whispered.

"The Johnny Cash song? *Awesome*," said Craig. He and I were camped out in the middle of the crowd with Kaya, Cat, Tess, and a few of Craig's hockey buddies, who, turns out, were pretty cool. Cat's crush on Craig's teammate, Nick Horne, had continued to bloom, and she now acted like she thought hockey was the most intensely interesting activity known to humankind.

"Well, *I'm* partial to the Red Wings, but I guess the Kings aren't bad," she flirted as Tess and Kaya rolled their eyes in my direction.

"She is so gone," Kaya groaned.

"Well," Craig said, eyeing his pal, "the girl's got great taste."

"Not as great as *mine*." I fake swooned and threw my arm around my new boyfriend's neck. He had a dark mottled bruise on his right temple where Duff had punched him, but otherwise he was no worse for wear. The bump on the back of my head was still tender, but not visible.

"Get a room, you two," Tess teased. "And Craig, maybe you should find some concealer while you're at it."

"Yeah, man," said Kaya. "Was Duff wearing brass knuckles when he did that?"

"I can't believe they're cutting this huge sucker down," I said, trying to change the subject while eyeing the giant evergreen.

"Our ancestors would be having a conniption fit," said Cat, taking a break from her flirting long enough to recognize the injustice.

"There are things that are right in this world and things that are wrong, and it's up to people to choose," I weighed in, feeling mildly indignant as I took a few last photos of the majestic landmark. "That anyone on this stupid planning committee could convince themselves that this is the right thing to do means they are deluding themselves."

"But the plans are already in motion," Craig said. "I agree with you, in principle, but that train has left the station. It's not like they can do anything about it now."

"Aren't you and I living proof that it's never too late?" I reminded him. "It's certainly never too late to do the right thing. I mean, look how beautiful this tree is! Isn't anything sacred anymore?"

"Now you're talking Yup'ik," Tess said, stifling a laugh.

"Or maybe she's channeling Jenna," said Kaya.

"Speaking of," said Nick, his eyes gazing past us, "here's your girl now." We all glanced in the direction Nick was looking and saw Jenna marching in front of a battalion of what looked like . . . wait, what was that?

"What are they all carrying?" Kaya echoed my sentiments as we squinted into the harsh noontime sun. Having amassed a brigade of at least twenty students and some local citizens, Jenna's Green Team was marching from the far side of the quad toward us. Each student held a posterboard with what looked like construction paper leaves pasted onto it. They were shaking and rustling the poster boards en masse while yelling a still unrecognizable chant.

"It looks like we're being attacked by a grove of angry trees," said Sean Stax, who braced his tall frame in front of Kaya and Tess. "Don't worry ladies: I'll protect you!"

"Who's that next to her?" Kaya wondered, jumping to see over Sean's shoulder.

"It's Duff," answered Craig. His voice—and his body language—had suddenly tensed up. I glanced at him inquisitively but he kept staring intently at the oncoming "forest" of students. By this time I could see Jenna and Duff more clearly. Both wore wild wreaths of pine branches on their heads and their faces were covered in camouflage war paint. Their militant rag-tag crew was similarly decked out, and they all chanted passionately.

"*SAVE THE TREE OR YOU'RE NEXT! SAVE THE TREE OR YOU'RE NEXT!*"

The whole student body soon picked up on the chant, although I personally thought the implied threat coming from the protesters was a bit heavy-handed. The chant grew more impassioned now.

"*SAVE THE TREE OR YOU'RE NEXT! SAVE THE TREE OR YOU'RE NEXT!*"

Craig dropped his hand from around my waist, and I turned to find him looking like he was about to puke.

"What's wrong?" I said quietly. He only shook his head in response, staring at his feet. Jenna and Duff broke away from their army of dissenters now and approached the stage in their strange foliage fashion statements. Principal Schaeffer stepped forward to stop them, but their body language made it clear they would be heard from before they accepted their punishment for humiliating the administration. The rest of the protesters waited off to the side of the stage, rattling their leave-bedecked posterboards, the sound of which lent an ominous drama as Jenna took the microphone.

"Distinguished friends, teachers, fellow students," she said, looking like the queen of the woodland sprites with her petite frame and limp, light-brown tresses. The poster-rattlers were subdued at the sound of her commanding voice. "We stand before you today as a coalition of diverse beings united in one cause: to save nature before we destroy ourselves. This majestic tree, in all her arboreal splendor, has been alive longer than all of us—before the cornerstone of this edifice was ever laid, before the earth under our feet became American soil, before our grandparents' parents took their first breath of air."

"Heavy," whispered Cat.

"She is sooo busted," Kaya added. I had to agree; Principal Schaeffer looked steamed.

"The forward march of time brings progress," Jenna continued, "but as we, the students of East Anchorage High, get ready to embark on our own future, we take one last stand to preserve the best, the most ideal, the most consecrated emblem of our past. Please do not pave paradise to put up a parking lot."

Jenna stepped aside now and yielded the microphone to Duff, who nodded as he positioned himself sternly at the podium.

"Yesterday is ashes. Tomorrow wood. Only today the fire shines brightly," he began, reading from index cards. "That's a native proverb, and it rings true for the cause that brings us here today. The memories that we seniors have created over the last four years are only that: memories, like dead leaves that wither and disintegrate. We don't know what the future will bring us as we go on to carve out our lives. But today we can choose to flourish. And so we must act."

"Well, they *are* building a theater," Tess said. Nobody laughed, and by her facial expression, even she realized it was a bad pun.

"The mistakes we've made," continued Duff, "the mistakes we are certain to commit in the future. . . . They're beside the point this afternoon. But the mistake we're about to make in destroying this testimony to God's grandeur is one we can't allow!"

The students erupted into a fit of applause, while the adults surrounding Schaeffer stood silently, looking like they had all just smelled a rotten egg that had been baking in the sun for hours.

"This tree nourishes us. We learned that in biology class, thanks to Mr. Gallagher," Duff went on. "It releases oxygen, which we need to exist. This tree has done its small part to keep us alive. If we cast aside Nature, we may not feel the consequences in this generation or the next. But mark my words: if we cast aside Nature, Nature will ultimately cast *us* aside. And so it is with one last heartbroken plea that we humbly ask you, Principal Schaeffer, and you, esteemed members of the school board, to reconsider removing this stately companion to countless graduating classes. Save the tree . . . or you're next. Save the tree, or we *all* will be next."

In my peripheral vision I noticed Craig's hand graze his cheek. Was he crying? Duff's speech was poignant, sure, but I didn't peg my boyfriend to be such a tree-hugger. Still, he was most definitely misting up, so I gently rubbed his back without looking at him or saying anything.

Having said their piece, Craig and Jenna returned to their throng of protesters, seemingly acknowledging that regardless of their attempt, they could not stop Old Burny from literally getting the axe. Principal Schaeffer looked vexed and unnerved as he returned to the mic.

"Mr. Wallace, Ms. Powell, thank you for your stirring speech. Er, uh . . . you raised a good point, which is why I am so pleased to point out that one hundred percent of Old Burny's pine cones, branches, bark, and roots will be salvaged and put to good use. Not one pine needle will go to waste."

"Tell it to the paper mills," yelled a guy from the back of the student section.

"In fact," Principal Schaeffer said, "the wonderful trunk of this tree will be carved into a totem pole next year by our art students, under the supervision of Mr. Ted Richter, to honor the native Alaskan cultures. It will be displayed proudly in the lobby of our state-of-the-art auditorium, where students and our very generous financial donors will be able to marvel at it and remember the stately tree it once was."

A number of boos emanated from my section of the crowd. Schaeffer's attempt at sprinkling sugar on this shitty situation wasn't working.

"Wait here." Craig broke free from our group and weaved his way toward the front of the crowd of students congregated on the lawn.

"Dude, where's he going?" said Nick, shooting me a bewildered glance. Craig stood a few feet in front, facing the podium.

"Principal Schaeffer, you've raised a really terrific point," he proclaimed loudly as he emerged from the crowd and walked toward the dais. I noticed he didn't seem teary-eyed anymore. Resolute was the better word. "If I may, I'd love to elaborate on what you've just suggested."

It was pretty evident that trying to stop all six-foot-two of Craig MacKenzie would be way more trouble than letting him have his two cents, so Schaeffer mustered a tight smile and ushered Craig to the podium as if it was his idea all along. Just as they'd listened thoughtfully to Duff and Jenna minutes before, my fellow classmates waited with bated breath for their Prom King to weigh in. I cringed, remembering what he'd said the last time he had a captive audience. All I knew for sure was, this wasn't really about the tree.

Craig cleared his throat before lowering his head closer to the microphone.

"Principal Schaeffer is right," he began, hesitantly. "We ought to pay tribute to this tree. But totem pole or not, it's inevitable: people will forget. When you destroy something so strong, cut it down in its prime, people mourn . . . for a while. But the memory soon fades. Future graduating classes will never know that a tree once stood here. It'll show up in photographs from time to time,"—here he caught my eye in the crowd—"but we won't be able to sit under its shade or enjoy watching the birds that nest here. I used to think that forgetting was the path to healing, the path to forgiveness. But I was wrong."

As if on cue, the birds were chattering overhead, giving his words more relevance. This time next week, there'd only be the sound of construction equipment.

"I don't know if I truly valued the meaning of life until recently," Craig said. "We all were affected by death in a profound way this year when we lost our classmate, Duncan Shaw." Although he barely flinched at the mention of his late son, I could sense by the look on Edward Shaw's face that the subject still caused him profound pain. Did he realize that the person responsible for his son's death was now addressing him?

"Mr. Shaw, I know that you will never forget Duncan. But I want you to know that I won't forget him, either. And I'm sorry. . . . He should still be alive, and he would be if only. . . ."

Craig placed both elbows on the podium and leaned over it as if he'd just been punched in the gut. He took a deep breath to collect himself before raising his head again.

"Duncan is gone, and there's nothing that can bring him back. But we can give him a much more fitting tribute than a dance routine in the gym and a few pages in the yearbook. This school is the last place where Duncan shone in his all-too-brief life. Sure, we can go to a cemetery and visit his grave, but wouldn't there be something more joyful and life-affirming about coming and sitting under this old tree and being surrounded by laughter and friends and youth: the very things that best represent him? I propose that we honor Duncan's memory by dedicating this tree to him with a memorial plaque. Let Old Burny remain standing as a testament to *his* life."

Of course, the crowd of students erupted into applause at Craig's suggestion, while the adults on the stage looked uncomfortable. Craig had really put them in an awkward position now. Would anyone be able to veto this idea with Duncan's still-grieving father present?

Duff and Jenna began leading the crowd in a brand new chant: *"SAVE THE TREE! DO IT FOR DUNCAN! SAVE THE TREE! DO IT FOR DUNCAN!"*

It occurred to me that Craig might have more to say on the subject of Duncan, so I was relieved when he backed away from the microphone and stepped off the stage, weaving his way back toward me. Through the din of the chants, Duncan's father, Edward, approached Principal Schaeffer, and several other members of the school board joined them in a discussion. After a few minutes, the crowd quieted, but the adults on stage were still mired in conversation. Finally Principal Schaeffer nodded his head and returned to the podium.

"The school board has decided to convene for a meeting this weekend to explore our options with regards to Mr. MacKenzie's suggestion. And so, since it looks like our dedication ceremony has come to a startling, er, impasse, I'd like to invite everyone to please partake of the punch and baked goods that members of the PTA have provided in the gymnasium." Schaeffer could barely hide his annoyance but I noticed that Mr. Shaw looked thoughtful. Craig had found his way back to me by now. He smiled but looked uneasy as we followed the crowd migrating toward the gym.

"Uhh. Way to go?" Tess said, staring at Craig wide-eyed as she walked backward in front of us. "What's next? Parting the Red Sea? Turning water into wine?"

"Seriously," Cat said. "Only a serious a-hole would chop down that tree now." Nick slung his arm casually over Cat's shoulder. "Were you planning it all along?"

"Let's just say a wise woman once told me I'd never have to worry about 'a single tree,'" Craig said, nudging Kaya in the ribs with his elbow. "I finally decided she was full of shit."

"Okay, wise guy!" Kaya said with a laugh.

Duff came jogging alongside us to catch up.

"Craig! Brilliant speech."

"Thanks man."

"Did I do that?" he pointed to the bruise on Craig's temple.

"Believe me," Craig said. "I deserved it." Duff looked confused.

"Well, anyway, no hard feelings, man," he patted Craig on the shoulder. "I had you pegged all wrong. I'm really sorry."

"Sure."

When we entered the gym, Craig grabbed me by the hand and pulled me away from the crowd. We found ourselves secluded under the bleachers.

"My herooooo," I comically sighed, leaning in to plant a kiss on him. I was startled when he pulled away.

"Don't say that." He was holding me affectionately around the waist, but he was deadly serious as I looked into his eyes.

CHAPTER TWENTY-SIX

Two Truths Are Told,
As Prologue to the Swelling Act

IT WASN'T FAIR. Four days wasn't enough time to reign as Craig MacKenzie's girlfriend. Whatever he was about to say to me, I knew it would ultimately change the trajectory of our relationship forever. Was he dumping me? No . . . I knew deep in my heart it was something much worse.

"What's wrong?"

He sighed and his voice quavered a little as he answered. "I need to tell you something. It's bad. As soon as I say it, things will never be the same. I've been lying to myself for months, but I can't lie to you. Not anymore. You're too good a person to love someone who did what I did."

His words sent a rippling ache through my body that started in my throat and fanned out into my limbs. Craig looked startled when I instantly started bawling and trembled from head to foot, but he continued to confess.

"Duncan's dead because of me. God," he said, bowing his head, "that sickens me, to say it out loud. I never told anyone. I should have come clean about it from the very beginning but I was just too afraid. I'm still afraid. But living with my conscience is worse."

"Craig, no." But he hadn't finished what he was saying.

"It's still all a blur, but I did it. We were out in the woods and I hauled off and punched him and he stumbled . . . he struggled with Beth . . . I can still hear his scream when he fell through the—"

"No!!!" I cried, throwing my arms tightly around his neck to stop him from saying anymore. "It was just an accident!"

"Sweetie, you have no idea—"

"Yes I do!" I said, sobbing as I clenched his forearms with my fingers. "I've known this whole time. Beth was the one who messed everything up!"

"She didn't mean to push him . . . it all happened so fast, and we didn't know the ice was so thin." I couldn't believe my ears.

"What? Beth was the one? What do you mean, she pushed him?"

"You don't understand. I thought Beth was the victim. She had just told me that night—swore, in fact—that he had tried to force himself on her."

"What?!" This was entirely new information.

"Duncan tried to tell me the truth, and deep down I knew he wasn't capable of that, but I wouldn't listen. Instead I punched him. Only when Duff came back, on prom night, did I finally realize she was lying. I should have known all along."

"So it's not your fault, then."

"Of course it's still my fault. I set everything in motion when I punched him. Beth went all spastic, and by the time he went in the icy water, it was too late."

"But it wasn't," I protested. "He was still alive! He froze to death hours later, not because you punched him, not because he fell through the ice, but because Beth swore you to secrecy."

Craig's head hung low, the shameful admission that everything I said was correct. He eventually lifted his gaze to meet mine.

"How do you know all this already?"

"I overheard you that night," I said. "I was in the backseat of your car. And then the following Monday at school I heard the two of you arguing about what had happened. Beth filled in the rest during our run-in at the movie theater. I didn't know about her false accusation against Duncan."

Guilt washed over Craig's face and he brought both hands to the back of his head, pulling at his hair in frustration.

"And you never said anything? Not to me? Not to anyone?"

I shook my head, tears still streaming down my cheeks.

"That makes me even more of a criminal." He held my neck in his strong, warm hands. "I'm so sorry. God, I didn't think this could get any worse."

"Quit talking like you're some murderer!" I said in a loud whisper. "You're not! What if someone overhears us?" Craig's face was still filled with self-loathing, but he looked more concerned for my feelings than for his own grim fate.

"It doesn't matter, because I'm turning myself in. I don't want to leave you, but I need to pay for what happened."

I leaned my forehead against his chest, sobbing.

"There's nothing you can do for me now," he said. "And you can't worry about me. You need to just go on with your life and be happy and find someone else."

"Me. Find someone else? Now I know you're losing it."

"I've never been more certain in my life."

"But what about Beth?" I said, pleading with him. "*She* pushed him into the icy water. *She's* the one who really bears the guilt of his death. She's the one who swore you to secrecy."

"But I didn't have to go along with it! I was just so freaked out, and so used to following her lead . . . anyway, there's no excuse," he finally continued. "Duncan would be alive and graduating with us this weekend if I'd just told the truth. Maybe it was an accident, but I *did* kill him, by saying nothing. He was my best friend . . . other than you, I mean. I didn't do the right thing then, so I have to do it now. Besides, believe me, Beth is already suffering enough."

As I wiped the snot from under my nose and gasped in small spasms to bring oxygen into my lungs, I didn't know how to respond. It would make me no better than Beth to try to talk him out of this decision. I knew, on a commonsense level, that telling the truth about that night was the only answer. It would certainly destroy him if he tried to harbor this secret for the rest of his life. But my heart was broken to shards knowing that this conversation would probably be our last before the repercussions—I shuddered to think what they might be—ripped us apart.

"So what now?" I sighed through my teary hiccups as he held me tight against his chest.

"Now, I go and have a chat with Chief Towers," he said. "Whatever happens, I'm willing to take it. I strangely already feel a little bit of relief having told you . . . it's like I'm finally on the path to making things okay again. Or at least being able to look in the mirror every morning and not despise myself."

"Don't ever say that," I said, hugging him closer. "I knew everything and I still loved you. I love you even more now."

"I love you, too. I'm going to miss you."

"Don't talk like that!"

"Skye, please. I need you to understand the reality of this. What I'm going to do now I need to do on my own. And I need to know I'm not ruining your life, too. Please. I'm not going to tell anyone that you knew anything about this. If you love me, you'll do me this one last thing. Just walk away."

I was weeping uncontrollably now, thankful that we were hidden away under the bleachers while everyone else in the gym was flittering around eating lemon bars and oatmeal cookies. It hurt so much to breathe. He gave me one last lingering hug and a kiss to end all kisses. Finally, he inched his face away from mine, pried my arms off his neck, and gave me one last tender kiss on the forehead. He was going to walk to the parking lot, get in his Jeep, and drive straight to the police station. He made a halfhearted joke about not getting permission to leave school early, trying, without success, to lighten the mood.

"I think I have bigger problems to worry about than detention." It was the last thing he said to me. I slid to the ground in emotional exhaustion as I watched him exit the gymnasium doors.

• • •

Whoever said it's better to have loved and lost than never to have loved at all was a moron. After trying to wipe off my face with Kleenex and pull myself together so that I could somehow feign allergies if anyone asked me what was wrong, I, too, made a bee-line for the exit and continued in a sprint-walk to the art annex. Fortunately, my puffy eyes and splotchy face received only a few perplexed glances from a handful of stray students before I locked myself away in the darkroom. I sat on the stool and hunched over the counter, letting the chilly Formica cool my flushed cheek. Fifteen minutes later, the buzzing of my cell phone jolted me out of my catatonic state. A text from Tess:

"OMG. Did U2 really get a room? Ha ha." She obviously thought Craig and I were off on some romantic romp. Not much later I heard students shuffling back into the art room on the other side of the darkroom door. Guess that meant our final class of the day was back in session. I was missing physics, but we were only playing with Slinkys today to review transverse and longitudinal waves. In other words, Mrs. Kimball was phoning it in along with the rest of us this late in the school year.

I could tell by his exasperated murmurs that Mr. Richter was having similar difficulties getting the juniors in his watercolors class to buckle down as I listened to his halfhearted lecture through the closed door. His voice reminded me that my senior art project was due in two more days. Trying not to make a sound, I swiveled on my stool to look at the posterboard photo collage leaning on the floor in the corner. I'd been agonizing over it for the last few weeks, but I knew it was pretty much crap. Ever since prom, I'd devoted approximately zero time to completing it, preferring instead to spend every waking minute hanging out with, talking on the phone with, or texting Craig. Craig! He was probably down at the police station by now. Perhaps Chief Towers had called his parents. Hopefully, they knew a good lawyer. It would be only a matter of hours before the news spread across town. I wondered if they'd show him on the local evening news, a sea of reporters crowding around him as he exited the station, holding up a jacket to shield his face from the cameras. Or maybe he'd be held in some terrible jail cell to await arraignment, or whatever it was called.

Using all the restraint I could muster not to text him to ask if he was okay, I stared at my collage in disgust. I'd basically just taken a glue stick and some scissors and gone to town with a bunch of old photos from the *Polar Bear Post,* sprinkling in scrapbook sticker words like "friends," "learning" and "fun!" It wasn't art, and it certainly didn't sum up my high school experience. I knew it would probably earn a nice, safe, "B-is-for-boring" from Richter, who would be disappointed but would ultimately let it slide. But what bothered me most was the fact that all the projects were going to be on display at graduation. I was irked with myself for not making a better effort. It would be humiliating to see this flimsy posterboard revealed to the entire graduating class and their relatives.

Of course, graduation was really an afterthought in light of everything that had just happened with Craig. I reflected on the dreaminess that was prom night. It was pretty much the only perfect memory that I had with respect to Craig, and even that was fraught with drama galore, what with Duff busting Craig's head open and Beth coming at me with a knife. But it wasn't the hype of prom night that stuck with me, or even our first kiss in the hotel basement. Instead, I kept replaying in my brain the quiet conversation I'd had with Craig in the hotel lobby before he got crowned Prom King. I could kick myself now, for being so stupid and shy with him. If I had behaved differently, he might not have ended up as Beth Morgan's boyfriend. He might not be currently facing a felony, for that matter. And it was all because I was too afraid to expose my true feelings to him, put myself on the line, step out of my comfort zone. I wasn't just disappointed in my photo collage. I was disappointed with what it represented. Until very recently, I never really had a true "high school experience," because I was too busy running away from it.

The school bell rang, and a dissonant clamor of sliding chairs, shuffling feet, and chatty *arteests* let me know that the watercolor class was vacating the room. Desperate to find out anything I could about Craig, I only waited twenty seconds or so until I thought the room was entirely empty. But when I emerged, a friendly voice surprised me.

"Ms. Kingston! Fancy seeing you here!"

Mr. Richter was stuffing a file folder into his beat-up leather briefcase. He ran one hand through his thinning blond hair and gave me an accusatory smile. One eyebrow was raised waiting for me to explain myself.

"How long have you been camped out in there?"

"Just for the last period," I said, hastening to explain myself. "We were only playing with Slinkys in physics, so—"

"*Slinkys.* Oh I see. Well, that would explain everything." He gave me a wink to let me know he was just teasing. With only three days of school left, apparently he wasn't too concerned about whether or not I was skipping class.

"Working on anything interesting in there, or were you just catching some Zzzs?"

"Well, I was working on my senior project," I said, fudging a little.

"And how's that going for you?"

"Mm. It's not."

"The attempt, and not the deed, confounds you. I'm sure it'll be wonderful," he said, making me cringe as I thought about my half-assed masterpiece. Mr. Richter held one of the heavy metal doors open and motioned for me to exit ahead of him into the bright sunshine. "If you're really stuck," he said, "stand on your head." I looked at him as if he'd just told me he liked to eat small children in his spare time.

"I don't mean literally. It's a little trick I have when I'm creatively blocked. I try to turn things upside-down, or inside-out in my head."

"Uh, okay. Thanks." Whatever.

"And, Miss Kingston?" he added, before taking his leave. "I know there's less than a week of school left, but don't let me catch you hiding out anymore."

I meandered my way back into the main school building heading for my locker. Despite the energetic buzz from other students that was in keeping with the end of the school year, nothing else seemed particularly unusual. I wondered if Craig was being fingerprinted now, or getting his mug shot taken . . . staring blankly into the official police camera as the flash bulb exploded before his dazed and confused face. The thought filled me with intense sadness, but it also gave me an idea. With Mr. Richter's final warning echoing in my head, I ditched the heavy books in my messenger bag, grabbed my camera, and slammed my locker door shut. I dug for my phone in my bag and returned Tess's text.

"Need yr help ASAP for Richter project. Tell the girls."

Glancing down the hall, I saw Brett Sanders and Kristy Winters milling around by the drinking fountain.

"Brett! Kristy!" As I hurried in their direction, the look on their faces made it clear they were surprised to be summoned by the likes of me. "I need your help. How good are you at taking pictures?"

CHAPTER TWENTY-SEVEN

When Shall We Meet Again?

"HOW'D MY PICTURE TURN OUT?" Lenny leaned past Tess and whispered to me as we waited in line to go onstage, his royal blue silk gown rustling in the light breeze that swept across the football field.

"You'll just have to see for yourself," I said.

"But did it look good? I mean, I know *you* looked good, but I couldn't figure out if I was completely in focus or not on that antique camera of yours."

"Shhh. Don't worry about it. Get back in your spot, it's almost time!"

"By the way, congratulations."

"You, too, Lenny."

"*SKYE KINGSTON. . . .*" Miss Hen announced my name, so I climbed the risers and headed over to shake hands with Principle Schaeffer. He handed me an empty leather diploma case—the real certificate would eventually come in the mail, so this was just for show. Nothing is ever quite what it seems.

"Well done, Skye."

"Thank you, Mr. Schaeffer."

"*RYAN KOWALSKI. . . .*" I stopped at the designated spot in front of the American flag to get my professional photo taken, as if I really wanted a visual keepsake of myself in this elephantine gown and mortarboard cap.

"*GINA KRUGER. . . .*" I craned my neck to see my parents, who were sitting in the grandstand with Ollie in the family section. Mom waved like a freak while Dad frantically snapped pictures on my camera.

"*TESS LITTLEFISH. . . .* " Tess beamed brightly as she, too, shook Principle Schaeffer's hand. She held her diploma case up in the air like it was the Heisman Trophy.

"*LEONARD LIVERMORE. . . .* " Filing back down the stairs and into my row of seats, Cat looked back at me and gave a raise-the-roof gesture. She was already in party mode, and I knew she was just itching to whip out the can of neon orange Silly String she had hidden under her gown. Jenna was going to have a coronary, but oh well.

"*BREE LUNDQUIST. . . .*" Before I had a chance to sit down, a wayward beach ball bonked me on the head. The crowd was getting restless. The speeches and award presentations had taken an hour, and now the calling of the names was dragging. Everybody was chatting and goofing off with friends, and nobody was paying much attention to the official proceedings on stage. At least, not until his name was called.

"*CRAIG MACKENZIE. . . .*" Maybe I was just ultra-sensitive, but I thought I sensed a hush come over the crowd. Regardless, I was proud of him as he strode across the stage with his head held high. He looked hot, even with that dorky tassel swinging across his face. It was a minor miracle he was even here today—not that he was on Easy Street, by any stretch. There was still plenty of legal wrangling between the team of lawyers his parents had hired and the district attorney's office. But because he was cooperating with the police—and because Duncan's family had lobbied the school on Craig's behalf—he was allowed to walk at graduation with the rest of us. Innocent until proven guilty, after all.

Beyond paying him one brief visit at his folks' house (they were keeping him on a short leash, naturally), I hadn't had much opportunity to find out the latest. It hadn't made the local news the night he turned himself in. Not until the next morning did the *Daily News* report his name in connection with the case, and the local television news outlets had taken gleeful relish in the story ever since. He'd been arrested on the spot, and his family had immediately posted bail. There would eventually be a trial to decide his fate. Although he was likely to be charged with negligent homicide, I didn't know the particulars of his case, since it was all still being hashed out with plea agreements and lawyerly mumbo-jumbo. Various news outlets mentioned Beth in connection with the crime, and I was thankful that Craig hadn't thrown himself on his sword for her by taking all the blame. But it remained unclear what charges she would face for her part in the incident. After the night at the Regent, she'd been MIA, and I'd only recently heard reports that she'd been admitted to a psychiatric facility.

"Am ok all things considered," was the first text Craig sent me the evening after his arrest. The Shaw family had reacted as you would expect—with outrage and bitterness—when they found out their son's so-called best friend had abandoned him to die in the woods. Several days later, it was still a mystery why they had made the request that Craig be allowed to attend the graduation. One last concession, perhaps, before he was locked up for decades?

When Craig returned to his seat, I leaned over and peered at him down the row. He was waiting for my glance, proudly grasping his diploma holder in both hands. I smiled back at him, but it was a bittersweet moment for us both. Even before the day he saved Old Burny, I'd had my private doubts about whether he and I could ever really have a future together. I was moving to California in three months, and he'd been groomed since birth to attend whatever prestigious East Coast college his father had ordained for him. At the time, I'd thought about the possibility of a long-distance relationship. We could try to make it work, but what were the odds? If the door had been only open a crack *before* he'd gone to the police, that door was officially now shut. And locked. And barricaded with heavy, immovable objects. I loved him, but let's face it: it was all over before it had even begun. He most certainly would *not* be headed to college in the fall as things now stood. He'd be lucky if he even got a cell with a window.

The ceremony finally concluded with the marching band's rousing (but semi-out-of-tune) rendition of "Pomp and Circumstance." Even with the occasional miscues by the brass section, the song stirred up sentiments deep in my gut that I'd been trying to keep at bay all afternoon: feelings about a soulmate found and lost; parting ways with new friends; my parents' separation; memories of late nights with the newspaper crew; my reluctance to leave my baby brother; regrets that I was being forced to fly away, having only just tentatively broken through my shell.

Craig inched his way down the row of seats so that he was standing next to me. He grabbed me around the waist with one arm, and I hoped he couldn't see that I was on the verge of bawling. Apparently, he was feeling sentimental, too.

"We'll always have Paris," he sweetly joked, reminding me of when we'd gone to see *Casablanca* at the Regent that summer before our sophomore year.

"Neither of us even have passports," I ruefully pointed out.

"Okay, well, we'll always have the darkroom." He gave me a quick peck on the cheek before Principal Schaeffer invited us all to let our mortarboards fly. I flung mine as far as I could into the sky.

"Hasta la vista, fugly hat!" I heard Kristy Winters scream from two rows behind us.

Students milled around on the fifty-yard line, celebrating and posing for pictures together as friends and relatives emptied out of the bleachers. Jillian was filling in Duff about the fact that she was going to journalism school at Northwestern University. Kaya was lifting the hem of her graduation gown to show off the four-inch platforms she was sporting.

"I *thought* you seemed taller!" I heard someone behind her squeal.

"So you decided to behave?" I asked Cat, nodding to where she might have hidden the Silly String contraband.

"Are you kidding?" she laughed. "The last thing I need is Jenna on my case, harping about the ozone."

"You are a wise, wise woman."

People seemed to be keeping their distance from my scandal-plagued beau, but then Duff walked over with Kristy, who graciously asked to take a picture of Craig and me.

"Is that *eye shadow*, Skye?" she smiled as she steadied her digital camera.

"Baby steps," I said, my face reddening. One thing I would never need in my cosmetics bag was blush. A few more members of the cheerleading set skipped their way over to Kristy's side.

"I noticed Beth was a no show," commented one overtanned and underfed specimen named Natalia Frantz. Beth hadn't been at school since my encounter with her at the movie theater, and some wondered aloud if she'd been "institutionalized" again. Duff glanced at Craig, but before anyone could answer further, another pom-pom princess interrupted.

"Oh my god, Kristy, your earrings are so rad!"

"Really? They're my great-grandma's from when she was, like, a debutante or something."

As the girls delved into the finer points of their respective wardrobes and accessories, Duff and Craig had started talking about this season's hockey record. The topic of Beth had flown out the window, even though I, too, was curious as to her whereabouts. How ironic. Beth Morgan had officially been relegated to the one thing she feared most in this world: Obscurity.

Eventually, Craig gazed behind me about two feet above my head, his eyes expressing concern. I turned around to find my dad standing with Ollie perched on his shoulders.

"Hey!" I gave my mom a giant hug. Her eyes were misty.

"This one's been in Niagara Falls–mode for the last two hours," said Dad, nodding toward my sniffling mom.

"Yes, well, my baby girl only graduates from high school once," she said with a smile. "Besides, mister . . . I seem to recall you asking me to hand you a tissue or two."

I still, for the life of me, couldn't understand why these two were getting divorced. They seemed to have more chemistry now than ever before. I guess it was one of those things that would always remain a mystery—but I was happy, at least, to see them finally getting along so well.

They both shifted their eyes expectantly toward Craig, who stood nervously beside me.

"Oh, Mom, Dad, this is Craig." He cleared his throat and extended a hand toward my dad for a shake.

"Nice to meet you."

"We've heard *so much* about you." Uggh. Leave it to my mother to utter the most inappropriate string of words that could possibly have escaped her mouth.

"I've talked about you a lot," I said, hoping he understood that they'd heard a lot about him from *me*, not from the nightly news.

Craig fidgeted awkwardly, no doubt aware that my parents weren't too keen on the fact that I was madly in love with a would-be convict. A few days ago, I'd sat down with them and told them everything I knew. They expressed concern and sadness about Craig's situation, but I'm sure they weren't exactly thrilled. I'm not sure parents *ever* approve of the men their daughters fall for, but in my case, there was definitely some extra cause for alarm. Thankfully, they were extremely polite as we attempted some idle chitchat before Craig's own parents turned up to greet their son.

I hadn't seen Mr. MacKenzie since prom night at the Hurlyburly. Man, was the guy imposing. But today, he was dressed in an expensive-looking gray suit and he seemed surprisingly relaxed. Craig's mother was tall and graceful. I'd met her a few days ago at Craig's house. She now gazed at me with gratitude, as if thanking me for making her son's graduation day so normal and untainted. No one dared broach the topic of Craig's legal woes. Instead, his parents exchanged pleasantries with mine, until the topic of my senior art project came up.

"You guys have *got* to see Skye's photography," Craig said to his mom and dad.

"I'm intrigued," said my dad. "She wouldn't say a word about what she was working on!"

I got butterflies in my stomach at the mere mention of my senior project, which was on display with the other submissions in the art room. There was a notice in the graduation program inviting all the students and their families to check out the exhibition. We began the pilgrimage from the football field back to the art annex, and I couldn't help but notice that Craig's dad seemed particularly chatty, in a good way, with Craig. It surprised me, given the trouble he was in, that Mr. MacKenzie would be acting more teddy bear than tyrant.

As we crossed the parking lot, I heard someone yell my name. My mom's roomie, Margot, was exiting her car and waving her keys at me.

"Sorry I'm late! I couldn't find someone to take over my shift at the studio," she said.

"You only missed the boring part, anyway," I said. "We're just on our way now to go see it." I'd called Margot the day before and extended the invite, because I'd wanted her to see my photographs. Not only was I curious to hear her constructive feedback from an artist's perspective, I also needed her moral support in a big way. As it was, my hands were completely sweaty as we neared the art building, and I had nervous goosebumps running up and down my arms.

Stepping into the art room, I didn't even recognize it. Mr. Richter wasn't kidding when he had hyped our senior projects to be a big deal. It looked like a gallery now, not a high school classroom! The desks and shelving had been removed from the room, and all of the artwork was on display against white walls and white standing screens that had been set up at various spots in the room. There was even new track lighting on the ceiling that allowed each grouping of art to be spotlighted. Wow. The whole thing looked extremely professional, making me more relieved than ever that I hadn't turned in my amateurish posterboard collage.

We started at the entrance and worked our way around the perimeter of the room. Oil paintings and graphite sketches made up the bulk of the submissions, and they were truly impressive.

Jason Stern's drawing, *The Evolution of an East Anchorage Student*, was hilarious. It depicted a series of teenage male figures standing in profile. The first, on the left, was a depiction of a freshman Jason looking like a Neanderthal man, stooped over with a huge backpack, knuckles dragging on the ground. The final figure, on the right-hand side, showed Jason standing tall and proud in his graduation gown and cap, diploma in his hand.

"Now *that's* funny!" Mr. MacKenzie said.

Megan Riordan passed me as she was on her way out. "Skye, your pictures are fantastic, oh my god!"

I swallowed hard and thanked her, feeling anxious but proud at the same time. I had glimpsed my pictures on the back wall when we'd first entered the room. The anticipation was building as we slowly edged our way back to that area. Cat was standing with her parents in front of her own submission, describing her pen and ink drawing, a framed circle that was filled in with black tribal designs. It was a very arresting graphic at first glance, but when you gazed within the circle at the pattern itself, you could see various figurative representations worked into the detail. It was almost like looking at a puzzle from which images slowly emerged.

"See—there's an open book, and there are four figures dancing . . . and there's a raven—"

"Go Ravens!" said Craig.

"Hey, you guys!" Cat introduced us all to her parents, who were extremely cordial.

"And you are obviously the young lady associated with the photo project," said Cat's father. "I was very impressed."

"Yeah, Skye, there's a mob scene around your pictures over there."

I glanced behind me and Cat was right—I couldn't even see my photographs because they were blocked by a semicircle of students and parents. Oh god. This was freaking me out. We continued to wend our way through the crowd, each new painting or sculpture garnering new oohs and aahs.

"I love this one here," said Craig, pointing to a simple sketch by Ashley Davis, a petite brunette whose locker was next to mine this year. "Do you see how fine the crosshatching is here on the shading? That's not easy to do."

"It looks like you could just reach out and touch it," agreed his dad. "Practically three-dimensional."

"Exactly." I smiled to see Craig looking genuinely happy as he looked at all the art projects, and I was further encouraged to see him getting along so well with his dad.

We finally reached a bottleneck near the back of the room and had to actually wait our turn to inch our way in to see my pictures.

"Great job," said one stranger—someone's mom, I presumed—as she squeezed her way past me.

"Oh wow!" said Margot, who was the first to get close enough to see my wall of work. We all finally closed in upon my series of twelve framed black-and-white photographs. A small white index card near the bottom right of the grouping stated my name and the title of the series: *Exposure.*

"Skye . . . you look . . . stunning," said my mother. "This is amazing!"

My dad was speechless, but Ollie, still perched on my dad's shoulders, piped up, "Kye! Kye!"

There I was staring back at me in twelve different frames lined up in four rows of three. Under each individual portrait was the name of the student who took the picture. The first photo was a shot of me in the parking lot. The photographer, Brett Sanders, had lain on his back on the asphalt when he took the picture, so I looked about twelve feet tall because of the unusual perspective. I laughed to myself, remembering Brett rolling around and getting dirty on the ground as he aimed for just the right angle. The second picture was cropped tightly on my eyes. I had heavy eyeliner and smoky shadow on my lids, which made my light irises look sharp and piercing—cat-like, almost. The photographer, Kristy, had convinced me to add the makeup at the last minute, and I'm glad she did. It made all the difference in the shot.

"Not bad, if I do say so myself." I heard Lenny's voice behind me. The picture he'd taken of me was slightly out of focus, but the way my hair was blowing behind me in the breeze, it gave the image a mystical, surreal quality. "See," Lenny explained to Megan who was standing next to him. "I *meant* to be out of focus. This was exactly the look I was going for."

"Skye, these are . . . perfect," said Craig, grabbing my hand and squeezing it.

"Looks like something you'd see in *Vanity Fair*, that's for sure," agreed his dad.

"And, my dear, you look just so *lovely*," added Mrs. MacKenzie. My dad just stared at me with eyes wide open as if he was thoroughly bowled over.

"My sentiments exactly," said a friendly, familiar voice from behind me. I turned to see Mr. Richter introducing himself to my mother. "Wonderfully creative, Skye, and well executed."

"Really?" I said. "I was a little nervous, because, well . . . I obviously didn't take the pictures and I know it was supposed to be our own original work."

"But you conceived the concept and chose the final shots, and that's just as important. Great art is about thinking outside the box and putting yourself on the line. That's what I was hoping to get from you, and you didn't disappoint me."

He was right that I put myself on the line. As much as I knew the photos were visually stunning, I was still uncomfortable seeing these blown-up representations of myself on display for the entire world to see. I couldn't hide from them, and that was a scary feeling. It was equally uncomfortable having to trust other people with each shot. Giving up control was always tough—heck, it was tough even approaching some of the people I'd asked to take the pictures. There was the shy kid, Neil Banks, who had Asperger's syndrome and tended to stick to himself. I'd never said a word to him before this, and we didn't talk much during the shoot, either, but the picture he'd taken of me in front of a window turned out to be a huge surprise. I hadn't even known the streaming rays of sunlight were surrounding me until *after* I'd developed the film. The effect was downright awesome. Then there was Corey Parkman, the dude everyone chalked up as being a neo-hippie stoner. He was actually quite hilarious, and it was his brilliant idea to take a picture of me towering in the middle of a group of the shortest freshmen girls we could recruit. I looked like a giraffe lost in a herd of gazelles—too funny.

In just a few days time, I'd managed to meet dozens of new people at my school as I rushed to complete the photographs. With each new picture that was taken, I became more comfortable talking to new people; more comfortable in my own skin. I'd only ended up choosing twelve of the best photos for the exhibition, but I had posed for over forty different students in all. The project went a long way in helping to distract me from worrying myself sick over Craig, and as much as I had dreaded playing "model," in the end, I actually wound up having a lot of fun.

"Craig, when did you take this one?" his mother asked, pointing to a framed portrait of the two of us in the middle of the wall. In the shot, he and I were standing in front of a mirror in his house. He had my bulky old camera lifted up to his eye, obscuring his face, but I smiled peacefully next to him, resting my chin on his shoulder and gazing thoughtfully out of the frame.

"I took it just the other day when she was over at the house," he said. Nobody said much more as we continued to look at Craig's photo. Perhaps we were all thinking the same sad thoughts about his future. I sighed, feeling a mixture of pride, grief, hopelessness, and contentment. It was amazing that so many mutually exclusive emotions could cohabitate inside my brain at the same time. Craig's picture of the two of us wasn't the most unusual or the most artistic shot of the bunch, but I liked it best of all. The face looking back at me was reassuring, in a weird way. It's like the "me" in the photograph was speaking directly to the "me" who was in the art room and saying, "Everything's going to be okay after all." I didn't exactly know what made her the arbiter of my fate, but I decided to trust her. Like the Mona Lisa, she looked like she knew something I didn't.

CHAPTER TWENTY-EIGHT

Leave All the Rest to Me

AS THE ALASKA AIRLINES JET MADE ITS ASCENT above Anchorage, seeming to float between the clouds and the town that had been my home for all of eighteen years, I looked down at the streets and buildings below and then out at the awe-inspiring, mountainous landscape that spread beyond the borders of the city. How perfect—and how perfectly calm—everything looked from up above. It was a gorgeous day; billowy cotton-candy clouds hung in the bright blue sky as if suspended by invisible thread. At this speed the air practically cradled the plane. I loosened my grip on the charm I'd been clutching when the plane took off. Leaning back in my seat, I held up the crystal, and the glinting rays of light refracted, spraying across my lap and the seatback in front of me. Craig had pulled it from his pocket at the airport, saying that he'd gotten it as a reminder not to forget him. As if I ever could. I smiled to myself, remembering our last few moments together.

My parents and baby brother had been there to see me off. I said my goodbyes, kissing Ollie on the top of his fuzzy head, wondering how many words he would learn before I saw him again. It was everything I could do not to cry, but Mom was bawling enough for the both of us as we parted ways at the entrance to the security line. Even Dad looked like he was moments away from busting up.

"See you later, kiddo. Call us when you land," his voice wavered, before they headed back toward the airport entrance.

I was already corralled in line behind the x-ray machines when I heard my name.

"Skye!" It happened all the time, thinking I'd heard my voice when in reality, it was only a stranger yelling "Hi" somewhere across a crowded room. And yet, it had distinctly sounded like . . . but of course, it couldn't be. My mind was only playing tricks on me, no doubt because I'd spent the better part of last night thinking about him. But then I heard it again: My name. His voice. This time it was unmistakable.

"Skye!" I craned my neck, but I couldn't locate him anywhere among the dozens of people standing in line behind me. I grabbed the handle of my rolling suitcase and began to worm my way back through the queue, hoping I didn't set off any terrorist sensors in the process. He was waiting for me at the entrance to security.

"Young man, I cannot let you through here without a boarding pass and ID," said a militant TSA worker.

"It's okay, ma'am," I said, grabbing Craig by the hand and walking him over to an empty ticketing counter. My mind reeled.

"I can't believe you're here," I said, my eyes already starting to mist. He looked at me, and I could tell he was wondering if I meant that in a good way or a bad way. I'd grown used to the idea that it might be months, even years, before I'd see him again. After the plea agreement, he was pretty much under house arrest until he finished the terms of his lengthy community service. Craig and his family had been incommunicado during the last couple of weeks, but I wasn't surprised given the hounding they were receiving by the press. His dad had taken away his cell, and whenever I tried their home line I got a busy signal. I knew we'd talk at some point, I just didn't know when.

"I thought for a sec that maybe I shouldn't have come," he said. "That maybe you didn't want to see me."

"Are you crazy?" I scolded, wrapping my arms around his neck as he lifted me toward him in a bear hug. I held his cheeks in both my hands and pulled his face toward mine.

"Crazy? Yeah, a little," he laughed as he set me down after our kiss.

"What are you doing here?" I asked, pulling away. "I'm surprised they'd let you anywhere near an airport!"

"My dad and Mr. Shaw talked to the judge and the parole board, and they've decided to allow me some leniency." My eyes widened with incredulity.

"Okay, the parole board, I can understand," I marveled, "But your *dad?*"

"Yeah, I know. You and me both."

"But what do you mean, 'Mr. Shaw talked to the judge?' Why would he do that?"

"The Shaws are incredible people." Craig shook his head with an air of respect. "They said they discussed it and decided that they didn't want to compound the tragedy of what happened, well, . . . *that night*. Still, I don't deserve their mercy. Mr. Shaw had a long talk with my dad. Told him that there are things he wished he'd done differently with Duncan. Like not pushing him so hard with sports. The gist of it is that I don't have to go to law school anymore—not that I would've been accepted with my record, anyway. But can you believe my dad actually used the phrase, 'You should do what makes you happy?'"

"Unbelievable!"

"No kidding. For some reason, he seems to have really lightened up about the whole art thing, too."

"That's great!"

"I've been drawing a *ton* since I've been cooped up at home these past few months, and he thinks I should give it a go. So I'm thinking about trying to take some classes at the community college. Not USC like *you,* Miss Big Shot, but things are kind of working out."

"*Kind of* working out? Are you kidding? This is better than we could have ever hoped for!" I expected Craig to seem as gleeful about this news as I was, but his happiness seemed more measured.

"None of this alleviates my guilt—not by a long shot. Every day I think about what happened and how I'll never be able to make up for it."

"Flight two-twenty-three to Los Angeles boarding in thirty minutes at Gate C4," said the announcer over the intercom. Craig and I both stared at one another for a moment, knowing our time was running out. Once again, I longed for that pause button on the remote control of life. The lump forming in the back of my throat was acutely painful.

"Well, I guess this is it." Craig gently squeezed my hand.

"I don't want to leave you. Say the word, and I'll stay." I put my arm around his neck and leaned in for another kiss.

"You're getting on that plane. This is the right thing for you to do."

"How do you know?"

"Trust me. I just do."

"What if you're wrong?"

"Remember what your mom told you?" he said with a sigh. "Why she and your dad split up?"

"Because she still needed to follow her dreams."

"Exactly," Craig brushed my hair from my forehead and kissed it gently.

"So I need to do this now so we don't have to break up later?"

"Yep. That's exactly why."

"That seems ass-backward."

"Nonetheless. . . ."

"When will I see you again? My parents can't afford to fly me home for the holidays."

"I wish I knew, Skye," he said. "I've still got months of community service ahead of me . . . by the time I can visit, if I'm even allowed to visit, you may not want to see me," he trailed off.

"That's an impossibility," I argued. "I will always, *always* want to see you."

"The minute I can visit, I will. I'll find a way," he said hoarsely, pulling me to him for one last kiss. He practically suffocated me with a hug, but I didn't care. I never wanted to let go. "You'd better go, Beanpole," he said, holding me even more tightly. "You'll miss your flight. I love you. Oh! And here. . . ." He dug into the front pocket of his jeans and brought forth the faceted prism, dangling from a platinum chain. "So you don't forget."

Ding. The seatbelt sign switched off. I brushed a tear from my cheek and blew my nose with an Alaska Airlines napkin, then looked down at the crystal in my lap. It reminded me of the Crystal Gallery of Ice I'd seen last Christmas—a bittersweet thought. I hoped those ice sculptures—beautiful, but melting—wouldn't serve as a metaphor for my relationship with Craig. Would we be able to survive the distance? After everything we'd been through together, would time, space, and separate lives prove to be more than we could conquer? I felt like my entire senior year had been an emotional battle, and I still wasn't sure whether I had lost or I had won.

It felt scary to be hurtling forward toward the unknown, but Craig was right. I needed to do it on my own. As a stewardess walked down the aisle handing out headphones, I lifted the chain and put the crystal charm around my neck, tucking it away, inside my blouse where I could feel it always next to my skin. The plane kicked into full speed taking me farther away from home and toward my new life in California.

Come What Come May

IT WAS AFTER THREE IN THE MORNING when Skye finished her story, only to be met with a disturbing silence. She wondered if she'd bored her roommates to death—or at least to sleep—when suddenly the room erupted with a flurry of questions and comments.

"No way. Did he really turn himself in?"

"I wouldn't have. I'd have gone to Mexico, first. They'd have to catch me. I'd go into hiding . . . live in a shack on the beach."

"Right," said another. "I'd love to see you trade in your gourmet coffees and weekly manicures for that."

"But how could you just let that crazy bitch get away with it? Not to mention trying to filet you with a knife?" wondered the first.

"I don't believe it, anyway. You made the whole thing up, Skye." The skeptical voice from the bunk below Skye's retracted her comment after dodging a pillow lobbed in her direction. "Okay, okay, I believe it," she said, "but you have to admit it's pretty wild. If we knew you were chock full of *this* much drama, we'd be begging you for bedtime stories every night!"

"I wouldn't blame you for not believing me," Skye said. The glow-in-the-dark stars stuck on the ceiling above her bed had long since faded. "Sometimes it still doesn't seem real to me. Not any of it."

"Do you think you'll ever see him again?"

Skye rolled over and said to the wall, "Nevermind. It's late . . . or early. Let's get some sleep." She tugged her covers up over her head and pretended to sleep. She didn't want to talk about Craig anymore. It hurt too much.

After briefly shuffling in their respective sheets, Skye's roommates yielded to silence, and she eventually heard the even tempo of their breathing as they slipped one by one into slumber. She marveled at how she'd gone from being her dorm room's pariah to its celebrated phenom in the course of one long night. A year ago, she'd never have been able to reveal so many personal facets of her life to people she barely knew, people who might easily judge her. But now that she had laid all her vulnerabilities, triumphs, and heartbreaks out on the table, she suspected that her three roommates would be a little more approachable from here on out. Maybe they'd even grow to be friends.

Skye lay awake, watching the moonlight (or, more likely, the light from the megawatt streetlamp outside their dorm) refracted by the crystal she'd hung in front of the window on the day she moved in. There was only an hour's time difference between Los Angeles and Anchorage. Was Craig still awake and thinking about her, she wondered? Doubtful. They hadn't managed to find time to talk much and she'd finally stopped obsessively checking her phone for his texts. What was there to say? He was busy with community service and trying to figure out what he was going to do with the rest of his life. She was taking a full load of courses and completely immersed in her new world. Maybe it was for the best, she thought, as she punched her lumpy pillow into submission and rolled over, preparing to count sheep if that's what it took. Glancing down at the nightstand to check the time, she noticed the green light emanating from her phone. Reaching down, she picked it up and punched in her passcode. It was a text from Cat:

"Guess who I ran into today? Your favorite Prom King. My latest prediction: You're going to be receiving a visitor very soon. Just be sure to use your charms wisely!"

Leave it to Cat to be ambiguous with her advice—or was it another prophecy? It didn't really matter, Skye mused. Whatever the future held, one thing was certain: she wasn't afraid.